Mrs. Malory and a Necessary End

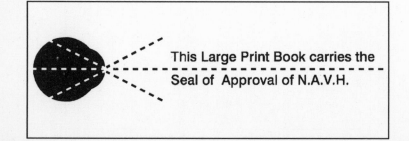

This Large Print Book carries the Seal of Approval of N.A.V.H.

A SHEILA MALORY MYSTERY

MRS. MALORY AND A NECESSARY END

HAZEL HOLT

THORNDIKE PRESS
A part of Gale, Cengage Learning

Detroit • New York • San Francisco • New Haven, Conn • Waterville, Maine • London

GALE
CENGAGE Learning®

LIBRARY OF CONGRESS CATALOGING-IN-PUBLICATION DATA

Holt, Hazel, 1928–
    Mrs. Malory and a necessary end : a Sheila Malory mystery / by Hazel Holt. — Large Print edition.
        pages cm. — (Thorndike Press Large Print Mystery)
    ISBN-13: 978-1-4104-5656-4 (hardcover)
    ISBN-10: 1-4104-5656-0 (hardcover)
    1. Volunteers—England—Taviscombe—Fiction. 2. Murder—Investigation—Fiction. 3. Large type books. I. Title. II. Title: Misses Malory and a necessary end.
    PR6058.O473M746 2013
    823'.914—dc23   2012046597

Published in 2013 by arrangement with NAL Signet, a member of Penguin Group (USA) Inc.

Printed in the United States of America
1 2 3 4 5 6 7 17 16 15 14 13

*For Geoffrey, who never
got to see this one*

CHAPTER ONE

"It's only for a couple of days a week," Monica said. "Well, three days actually."

"I really don't think —" I began.

"It's quite fun," she said brightly. "And such a good cause. I hate to let them down, but Julie really needs me — moving house with a new baby, and he was premature, you know; they were really worried about him, in an incubator for over a week. So you do see. . . ."

"Well, yes . . ."

"It would only be for a few weeks, a month at the most."

"Really, I don't know if I can."

"Jean and Wendy you know, of course; they're very nice. They'd be working on your days. And on the other days there's Margaret and Dorothy. Norma works every day — she's a bit full on but really splendid."

"But I've never done anything like that

before. They may not want me."

"Oh, they're absolutely desperate. Anyone would be welcome."

In spite of this doubtful assurance I finally agreed to take over Monica's duties at the charity shop, beginning on the following Tuesday.

"You must be mad!" Rosemary, my best friend, was never shy about voicing her opinion. "Tying yourself down like that. Anything might crop up — suppose Michael and Thea need you to look after Alice."

"Oh, I expect the people at the shop are quite flexible about exchanging days."

"Don't you believe it. Not with Norma Stanley in charge; she's dreadfully domineering."

"I don't think she's actually in charge. It's Wendy's husband, Desmond. He looks after things — a sort of supervisor, I think."

"Well he's no better — a total control freak. Honestly, Sheila, you're so feeble about saying no to people. Can't you get out of it?"

"Not really. Anyway," I said defensively, "it might be quite interesting."

Rosemary sighed. "Well, don't say I didn't warn you."

Rosemary's right, of course. I do find it difficult to say no (a reasonably active widow is considered fair game), hence my presence on far too many committees. Still, I told myself, it was only three days a week for a few weeks (well, a month), and the hours weren't too taxing so there'd be time for other things. Anyway, it would be something different, coming into contact with new people all the time. And as Monica said, it was for a good cause.

Nevertheless, as I approached the shop I did feel distinctly apprehensive. Monica was there to greet me, and Jean Lucas and Wendy Barlow were familiar and friendly faces. However, when Norma Stanley appeared from the back of the shop, I remembered with dismay that she was the new and difficult member just elected to the committee of Brunswick Lodge, the main center of social activities in the town. Denis Painton, our chairman, had taken me to one side after the meeting and said grimly, "We're going to have trouble with that one."

Certainly she was a formidable figure — tall, with the sort of short, impeccably cut gray hair that often seems to indicate a forceful personality. Her voice was not unpleasant but with just that edge to it that indicates a tendency to command. However, she appeared to be in a gracious mood.

"So very good of you, Sheila — I may call

9

you Sheila? We are all quite informal here; we work as a team." Monica moved forward, preparing to show me round, but Norma continued: "Now, I'll just give you a brief idea of how things work and then we'll find you something to do — nothing too complicated for your first day here. Monica will show you the ropes before she goes. Tomorrow I'll take you through all the health and safety procedures."

"So, what was it like?" Rosemary was on the phone almost as soon as I got in.

"Well," I said cautiously, "it's a bit early to say. It seems quite straightforward — unpacking the stuff that comes in and sorting it. I'm not allowed to use the steamer yet (that's *very* health and safety) and certainly not the till, which they seem to regard as something as complicated as the Enigma machine and not to be trusted to anyone without a degree in technology! Norma likes to keep an eye on that herself."

"Ah, the dreaded Norma. How did you get on with her?"

"She remembered me from the Brunswick Lodge house committee, so she wasn't *quite* as patronizing to me as she is to the others. Gracious, you might say. Queen to lady-in-waiting rather than queen to peasant."

Rosemary laughed. "Dreadful woman. She came across Mother at some coffee morning or other and made the mistake of talking down to her as if she were an elderly person — she soon got put in her place and kept well away from Mother after that."

"I wish I'd seen it."

"Mother said, What can you expect from someone who comes from the Midlands?"

"Oh dear. Well, they seem to be very well-off, and then he inherited this large house just outside Taviscombe from his aunt, which is why they moved down here."

"What's the husband like — a mousy little man?"

"No, actually, he's tall and rather distinguished looking. Obviously dotes on her. According to Denis, he jumps to attention every time she speaks!"

"Well, I wish you joy of her. I wonder how she gets on with Desmond Barlow — I bet there'll be some clashes there."

"I haven't seen him in action yet — he came in after I'd left, to collect the money and take it to the bank. I'm sure Norma resents that!"

I was to work in the shop on Tuesdays, Wednesdays and Thursdays (which would leave me a lovely long weekend, Monica

11

said brightly), and on the Wednesday Desmond came early while I was still there. Immediately the atmosphere, which had been fairly relaxed in spite of Norma's bossiness, changed. Jean and Wendy went over to the shelves at the back and began busily rearranging the books and DVDs, and Norma moved across and stood guard over the till as if defying him to come anywhere near it. I pretended to sort through the rack of blouses, keeping my ears open for any exchange.

"Who changed the window display?" Desmond asked brusquely.

"I did," Norma said, moving even closer to the till. "It was far too crowded with things. What one needs in a window display is one really *good* object that stands out and draws the attention, with other related objects carefully placed around it. I think you will agree that the new arrangement is very striking."

"I don't think you have quite considered what we are here for," Desmond said smoothly. "I'm sure a degree of sophistication, while admirable in Bond Street, say, is not really suitable for a charity shop in Taviscombe. You see, people are not concerned with the artistic values of a window display; what they actually want to know is what we have inside. So if you could very kindly put it back the way it was."

I held my breath and waited for Norma's reply. There was complete silence for what seemed like an age. Then she said coldly, "Very well, if that's what you want, naturally, since you are in charge, we will do so."

He smiled smoothly. "Thank you. Now if you have the takings ready, I'll get them over to the bank."

They both moved into the back room, and I looked across at Wendy to see how she'd taken her husband's remarks. But she had her head down, apparently intent on sorting out some paperbacks. As they came back into the shop, Desmond stopped beside Wendy and said, "Did you get my gray suit from the cleaners?"

"Well, no — they weren't open when I came in, and I had to queue for ages in the lunch hour with that parcel you wanted posted."

"Then perhaps," he said, "you had better go now before they shut."

Wendy looked appealingly at Norma, who raised her eyebrows and said, "It's not really convenient, but, of course, if Desmond wants you to . . ."

Wendy rushed to the door and went out without even putting on her coat. She was back a moment later, saying breathlessly, "Forgot my handbag!"

As the door closed behind her, Desmond gave a theatrical sigh but made no comment.

When Jean and I were getting our things together to go home, she looked around to see if we could be overheard and said, "Honestly, I don't know how she puts up with it — Wendy, I mean. It's awful the way he speaks to her, as if she's some sort of servant! He's always criticizing her — poor thing, he's destroyed any bit of confidence she's ever had."

"I was rather shocked," I said. "I don't think I've ever seen them together before."

"It's all right with someone like Norma. She can take it — and dish it out, too. That wretched husband of hers is another door-mat. But poor Wendy is such an inoffensive little thing, everyone feels sorry for her. Well, it wouldn't suit me!"

"Do you know Desmond Barlow?" I asked Michael when he came round to ask me if I'd collect Alice from the riding stables at the weekend.

"I've come across him in connection with a couple of charitable trusts — he's a great one for good works, on all sorts of commit-

14

tees and stuff, and I believe he's a lay preacher, too."

"Well, someone ought to tell him that charity begins at home," I said. "The way he treats his wife is abominable."

"He does have a great line in sarcasm. Not very pleasant, but he gets things done. An active retired man is always in demand, so people put up with his unpleasant manner."

"They're not local — where did they come from?"

"Somewhere in the Midlands, I think. He was some sort of civil engineer, used to laying down the law. Anyway, I'd better be going. I've got a site meeting in half an hour." He put the box of eggs he'd brought on the kitchen table. "Can you take another dozen? Now Thea's got these other hens, we're getting a bit overstocked."

I gradually got used to the work at the shop and (having been instructed in minute detail about the health and safety procedures) was allowed to wheel bags and boxes of contributions on the trolley and was grudgingly shown how to use the till by Norma ("It's because it's *electronic,* you see"), though I was not yet considered sufficiently advanced to use the steamer ("We have to be *very* strict about who uses it"). I found it was possible to cope with Norma by agreeing with everything she said, no matter what, and fortunately I had very little to do with Desmond Barlow. Norma did introduce us formally the next time he came in. When he discovered that I was Michael's mother (Michael being a useful contact), he treated me with a sort of smooth courtesy that I found more disagreeable than his sarcastic attitude towards the others.

Jean, who was very outspoken, had constant arguments with Norma, while Wendy kept her head down and obeyed Norma's brisk instructions meekly and without comment. She was the one who was best with the customers, endlessly patient and helpful with even the most difficult ones. It was Wendy, too, who noticed if you were feeling tired or stressed and appeared at your elbow with a cup of tea and a word of sympathy.

One day when I came back into the shop from the storeroom, I saw her talking to a young man. I couldn't hear what they were saying and didn't like to approach too closely because he seemed very agitated and she looked anxious and upset. I was a bit worried about them — some of our customers can be odd or difficult, and there was no one else in the shop. Norma had gone out ("I have to drive out to Porlock to collect some rather *good* items that Mrs. Forbes-Grayson has promised us"), so I went back into the storeroom to find Jean.

"There's a young man in the shop who seems to be upsetting Wendy," I said. "He's in a bit of a state. Should we do something?"

Jean came and peered round the door. "Oh no, that's all right. It's John, her son. He's at university — Durham, I think it is, or Nottingham, somewhere like that. I suppose he's back for the Easter holiday."

"Are they all right?" I asked. "They both seem very upset."

"Oh, he's a bit neurotic, if you know what I mean. Doesn't get on with his father — well, who would? He sometimes comes into the shop to talk to his mother. They can't really talk at home, not with Desmond finding fault with every word either of them says!"

"Goodness, how awful."

"It's not the way *I'd* like to live. I'll go and put the kettle on — she'll need a cup of tea, poor soul. It's usually about something unpleasant when he comes in like that."

I heard the shop door shut and went back in to find Wendy looking very distressed.

"Are you all right?" I asked tentatively.

She looked for a moment as if she was going to say something. Then she gave a wan

17

little smile and said, "No, I'm fine. Can you take over here?" and went into the storeroom.

I thought it would be tactful to leave her to Jean and the cup of tea that she obviously needed.

I asked Rosemary what she knew about Desmond Barlow.

"I've only met him a few times, at the occasional dinner party and so on. Not a nice person — always has to be right about everything and, like I said, a control freak."

"Michael says he's a great one for good works."

"That's as may be. It's all a bit ostentatious — 'look what a splendid person *I* am,' that sort of thing. Edna Palmer — you remember her, her son married Jilly's best friend' Susan."

"I don't think . . ."

"You must remember — she wore that hideous mauve outfit for the wedding — a designer label, she said."

"Oh yes, I do. And she went around at the reception telling everyone how much the wedding was costing them! So what about her?"

"Oh yes. Well, she goes to Desmond Barlow's church — the one he's a lay reader at — and she said he's offended a lot of the congregation, trying to take over too much from the vicar there. Poor man — the vicar, that is. He was grateful at first for the help — he's got three parishes to cover — but it's really getting out of hand, Edna says. The Barlow person is going around laying down the law about parish matters and organizing things without any sort of consultation, just as if he's the vicar of St. Mary's himself."

"I can quite believe it," I said.

"And he's got that wretched wife of his working her fingers to the bone with coffee mornings and things."

"I saw their son the other day; he came into the shop to talk to Wendy. It looked as if he was telling her something upsetting — she was quite distressed and looked awful when he'd gone."

"He's another poor soul, according to Edna. Apparently he's the artistic type, not at all academic, but his father somehow got him into Nottingham University to read law and he hates it and is really miserable."

"Oh dear, other people's lives!"

"Well, yes, but I do think Wendy Barlow might stand up for herself a bit more, for her son's sake as well as her own."

"I don't think she's capable of standing

up to anyone — she's just as bad with Norma. Some people just don't have it in them."

"I suppose so," Rosemary said doubtfully. Rosemary, bless her, is a great one for standing up for other people as well as for herself. "Actually," she went on, "Edna says they're having a coffee morning and produce sale at St. Mary's this coming Saturday — do you fancy going along to see the dreaded Desmond in action there?"

CHAPTER TWO

The church hall was quite busy when we arrived and most of the produce had gone, but Rosemary got some shortbread and a couple of tomato plants and I found a well-grown fuchsia that would go nicely in one of my planters. We located an empty table at the far end where the refreshments were being served, and Rosemary sat down while I went to get the coffees. Wendy was serving. She looked surprised to see me.

"Edna Palmer told us about it," I said, "and I can never resist a produce sale! It's being very well supported."

"Yes, we usually have a good turnout, and everyone works very hard to make it a success."

"The vicar will be pleased," I said.

"Oh yes — though, of course, Desmond organized it all. Mr. Nicholas — he's our vicar — has three parishes now and so many calls on his time."

"He must be very grateful for all the help Desmond gives. Edna was telling us how much he does."

"Desmond likes to keep busy."

"I must let you get on," I said. "I'm holding up the queue. I'll see you on Tuesday."

I'd just taken the coffees back to the table when Edna arrived.

"Well," she said as she pulled out a chair from one of the other tables and sat down beside us. "Fancy seeing you two here!"

"We thought we'd come and see how your Mr. Barlow is running things," Rosemary said.

"Running things is right," Edna said scornfully. "Telling Beryl Robinson, who's been in charge of the cakes for the past ten years, how she should arrange her stall! I can tell you, she nearly walked out there and then."

"Goodness!" I said.

"And Sybil Wells — she looks after the books and CDs — she said he insisted on going through all the books and changing the prices. Apparently he'd heard of someone finding a first edition of something or other that was worth a fortune. Sybil said it made her laugh to see him going through all the piles of Mills and Boone and Catherine Cookson, but then he found some old gardening book or other and took it away to look it up on the Internet."

"And was it valuable?" Rosemary asked.

Edna laughed. "No, of course it wasn't. He came back with it looking quite embarrassed, and Sybil gave him one of her *looks* and marked it, while he was there, at 50p."

"How splendid," I said.

"Is the vicar here today?" Rosemary asked.

"Oh no, he always keeps well away from things Desmond Barlow is organizing. Poor Mr. Nicholas. He's a nice man, but, really, with all he has to do these days — well, I suppose he's glad enough to have someone to help. And he's not the sort of person to *say* anything to anyone. Sybil said she was thinking of writing to the bishop, but as I said to her, you can't very well complain about someone doing too much in the parish!"

"I suppose it's better that someone does these things," I said, "rather than not have them done at all."

"That's as may be," Edna said, "but there's been a lot of umbrage taken. Mr. and Mrs. Williams have left St. Mary's and now they go to the Methodist church in the Avenue. And, mark my words, they won't be the last. It's hard enough to keep up a good congregation when that sort of thing is happening." She caught sight of someone across the room and stood up. "Excuse me, I must go and speak to Beryl about the Parish Breakfast."

"And I bet," Rosemary said, "that's being organized by Desmond Barlow as well!"

I laughed. "Where is he, anyway? I'd have thought he'd be keeping an eye on things, making sure everything's going to plan."

"There he is — over there, talking to that man with gray hair. They seem to be having some sort of serious conversation. The other man looks quite put out."

"Desmond laying down the law again, I expect."

"I don't know. It looks too personal for that. I wonder what it's about." She got to her feet. "I think I'll just go and have a look at those artificial flower arrangements."

"But you hate artificial flowers. . . ." I began as I saw Rosemary making her way towards the stall, which was near where Desmond and the other man were standing. People are always saying how inquisitive I am, but really, Rosemary's just as bad, and, when she's particularly interested in something, even more determined.

I watched with interest as she bent to examine some of the arrangements, but only a short while after she'd got there, Desmond broke away and went off towards the refreshment area, where he was obviously criticizing the way Wendy was stacking up the crockery.

Rosemary, having disappointed the artificial flower seller who'd felt sure of a sale, came back to our table.

"Well?" I said.

"No luck. They'd almost finished. But there really did seem to be something going on there."

"How do you mean?"

"For a start, I got the impression the man wasn't a parishioner."

"Perhaps he just wanted to buy a home-made cake or a potted plant."

Rosemary ignored my frivolous interruption. "There was definitely an atmosphere, some sort of tension between them. Desmond was saying, 'I think, however high they take it, they'll find it difficult to get anyone to take it seriously,' and the other man said, 'Don't think they'll let it rest there. It's too big a thing and too important.' Then Desmond went away and left the man before he'd even finished what he was saying."

"It was probably just about some committee business, nothing earth shattering."

"But the man was very angry. And Des-

25

mond, in spite of that unpleasant sneering manner of his, seemed quite shaken. There was a lot of emotion going on about whatever it was."

"There's a lot of emotion at Brunswick Lodge committee meetings," I said.

"No, but seriously, Sheila, I do feel it was something important."

"Oh well, we'll probably never know." I got up to join her. "Shall we go now? I think we've had all the excitement a church coffee morning can provide — whatever you think you heard. I must say, I thought you were going to have to buy that hideous beige-and-orange flower arrangement. It had feathers in it!"

Later, when I was tipping some old compost out of a planter to put in my new fuchsia, I did wonder what Desmond's conversation had been about. "However high they take it" and "Too big a thing and too important" — it did sound more than the usual committee exchanges.

Perhaps Rosemary was right. I began to wonder what other things Desmond was involved in as well as St. Mary's and the charity shop. Michael had mentioned some trusts; it could be something to do with one of them. Perhaps that was something I could find out about that might go some way to satisfying Rosemary's curiosity. My train of thought was broken when I realized that the planter I'd emptied had been invaded by ants. So I had to put it to one side and find another one for the fuchsia that I was now beginning to regard with dislike.

The next day I was having Sunday lunch with the children, and I took the opportunity to ask Michael a little more about Desmond Barlow.

"Like I told you," Michael said as he was putting out the table mats, "he's connected with a couple of charitable trusts — one's about providing low-cost housing for people and the other's about facilities for youth training — nothing spectacular. Why are you so interested, anyway?"

"Just because of working with him, really, and because of something Rosemary overheard at the St. Mary's coffee morning."

"Oh, if you and Rosemary are off on one of your wild-goose chases! Poor man, little does he know what dark forces he's unleashed."

"No, honestly, it was a bit odd — all about high places and things being too important to let rest."

"Come on, Ma. That could be anything."

"I suppose so, but still —"

I couldn't pursue the topic because Alice came into the room, carefully carrying a large salad bowl.

"Gran, Gran — I made it myself. I mixed the dressing and everything. Oh, and I helped Mummy make the trifle for pudding — I did the jelly and put the juice on the sponge cakes."

Alice is going through a cooking phase, which we are all naturally eager to encourage, though Thea, who bears the brunt of it, has said that she does wish Alice was as excited about washing up afterwards.

I told Rosemary, when she phoned later, that as far as I could see, there didn't seem to be anything sinister about Desmond's activities; the conversation at St. Mary's was probably just him being unpleasant as usual.

I had another opportunity to observe his unpleasantness on the Tuesday. I was putting out some more skirts on the rails when I saw Desmond outside looking in the window. He stood there for quite some time, occasionally writing in a small notebook. After a while he came into the shop and walked around, looking at the stock, making more notes and totally ignoring the staff and a couple of customers who watched him curiously. All this time he didn't say a word to anyone, and no one (not even Norma, who was at the till) said anything to him. After about ten minutes he went away.

Jean went into the back room, and I followed her.

"What on earth was that about?" I asked.

She filled the kettle and switched it on before answering. "Oh, that's his lordship putting us in our place."

"What do you mean?"

"It's to show us he's in charge and is keeping an eye on things. He does it from time to time."

"I was surprised Norma didn't say anything."

"She did the first time, but you know what he's like. He simply put her down. So after that, rather than be made to look a fool, she gave up. It's just one of his little ways — we don't take much notice now."

She stopped talking since Wendy, who'd been out to get some biscuits, came back. I was touched to see how neither Jean nor Norma seemed to make any sort of comment about Desmond when Wendy was there. I suppose it's because she's such a gentle creature and we all feel so sorry for her that it would (as I told Rosemary afterwards) be like kicking a puppy to be unkind to her.

Later on, when Norma was in the shop and Wendy had left early (some errand she had to do for Desmond), I said to Jean, who was in the back unpacking some bric-a-brac, "If Desmond's so horrible, why do you all stay?"

She put down a heavy cut-glass vase carefully on the table and thought for a moment.

"I suppose, basically, it's because we were here first and we don't see why someone like Desmond should drive us out. We enjoy working here; that's why we volunteered in the first place. Wendy is here because of him, of course, and Norma is tremendously keen on her social position in the town and she thinks that doing Good Works will give her an entree into Taviscombe society!"

I laughed. "I can see that, but what about the others?"

"Margaret never married and Dorothy is a widow and her only son is in New Zealand — they need the company. It's a bit like a family for them. Monica, as you know, was bullied into it initially by Margaret, but found she liked it and stayed on."

"And what about you?"

"Oh, I'm a golf widow — George spends every day down at the golf club, the children

30

are away and I got fed up stuck at home all day. I like Wendy and the others — Norma's a bit of a pain, but I can laugh at her, so that's all right. Besides, I think it's a good cause. Don't you?"

"Yes, it is. And I can see how none of you want to be pushed out of what you enjoy doing by Desmond's unpleasantness."

"Exactly." She took another object, a grinning china cat, out of the box and looked at it critically. "What a grotesque looking creature — who on earth would buy that? Certainly not a cat lover!"

I was getting into the swing of things at the shop and quite looked forward to going in now. I was interested in the customers — some hunting for a bargain (and there were some really terrific bargains), some "just looking round," and some (mostly visitors to the town) coming in out of the rain or looking for something to do when they had sampled the few entertainments the town offered. Then there were the professionals, looking for bargains that they might sell on or hoping (like Desmond) to find some valuable object underpriced because of ignorance — though with all the antiques programs on television, these days there's not much chance of that. And, anyway, Desmond had a couple of dealers in from time to time to value things.

Those are the interesting ones. There are some, though, you dread seeing — the disagreeable ones who try to beat you down over the price in an aggressive manner; some who are downright rude; the shoplifters, of course (there are always some of them); and the mad ones. There was one girl, about eighteen, perhaps younger — very thin, dressed in torn jeans and a grubby T-shirt, with long, tangled hair, a lot of heavy eye makeup, and piercings on her nose and eyebrows. She never bought anything but would roam round the shop, taking the garments off their hangers and leaving them draped over the rails.

"Keep an eye on that one," Jean said to me one day after the girl had prowled round the shop for a while and left. "We've never actually caught her taking anything, but I'm sure she does."

"Who is she?" I asked. "Do you know?"

"Oh yes, we know who she is. Her name's Sophie Randall."

"Randall? Nothing to do with Dr. Randall?"

"His daughter. It's very sad, really — she's been on and off drugs, run away from home twice, and goodness knows what else."

"How awful. Her parents must be desperately worried."

"Yes, I know all about poor Sophie," Rosemary said. "I've only met Dr. Randall a few times, but they have a younger daughter, Daisy, who's in the same class as my granddaughter Delia, so I see Mrs. Randall quite a bit at school things."

"They must be frantic — I know I would be."

"They've been through a lot. There was that time she ran away and was living in a really ghastly squat in Bristol — they found her through the Salvation Army, and Dr. Randall got her into some sort of drug rehabilitation scheme. Mrs. Randall hasn't said anything — naturally — but I think they're afraid Sophie is back on drugs again."

"Oh dear. She certainly looks terrible."

"Apparently she's been hanging around with a really unsavory young man, some sort of Goth, or whatever they're called, almost certainly on drugs and possibly a dealer. They've tried talking to her, but they're terrified that if they come down too hard on her, she'll run away again."

"What about the sister?"

"Daisy? The absolute opposite — works

hard at school, gold medal for the Duke of Edinburgh Award scheme, wants to be a doctor like her father."

"And what does she think about Sophie? Has she tried to help?"

"She tried, but Sophie just laughs at her and calls her a stupid little loser. Daisy used to be very fond of her sister, but now — so Delia says — she's just embarrassed, especially at school. Well, Sophie's a very visible presence around the town, and you know how unkind some schoolchildren can be."

"She looks so unhappy — Sophie, that is — when she comes in the shop. Jean says she's looking for something to steal and perhaps she is, but I can't help feeling sorry for her. And for her parents, too, of course."

"It doesn't seem fair. They've given both those girls the same love and attention, but then one turns out like that — there's no accounting for it."

"Goodness," I said. "It makes you realize just how lucky we've been."

"Count your blessings — that's what Mother is always saying when I complain. Mind you, the only things Mother counts are other people's defects."

CHAPTER THREE

Why is it that when a day starts badly, it always gets worse? I'd overslept, and when I got down to the kitchen I found that the animals had upset their bowl of water and Foss (a careless eater) had scattered half his food in the resultant mess. Tris, impatient for his breakfast, was pushing his food bowl around (making things worse) while Foss was weaving round my ankles as I tried to clear up, complaining about the delay in that particularly plangent Siamese wail. Unfortunately I wasn't wary enough, and he managed to nip my ankle (to make his point clear), so I had to spend precious time looking for something to stop the bleeding.

After that it was all downhill. Burnt toast, spilt coffee, laddered tights, mislaid car keys and, finally, my usual parking place unavailable because they were digging up the road. And, of course, when I did eventually arrive at the shop, late, out of breath and cross, I found Jean and Wendy ostentatiously busy at the front of the shop, Norma guarding the till and Desmond, who doesn't usually come in the morning, prowling around with his camera. I muttered some sort of general apology that he chose to ignore and went into the back room to take my coat off.

I was then confronted by the task I'd abandoned the previous day — a large black dustbin bag, half emptied on the floor. It may be the association of black bag and rubbish that causes some people to dump what *is* palpably rubbish on our doorstep as a so-called contribution. This lot was particularly useless: broken electrical equipment, chipped china and dog-eared books and magazines, together with a few crumpled, not-too-clean garments. I was just nerving myself to deal with this unsavory task when Desmond came in.

He looked with distaste at the pile on the floor and said coldly, "If you could kindly clear a little space so that we can get through."

"I was just going —" I began but he moved past me and started taking photographs of the locks on the window and the back door. Then he opened the door and photographed the guttering and the paving of the yard and the double doors that led

36

out into the alley beyond. As he turned to come back in, I hastily put on some rubber gloves and began to sort out the unpleasing objects before me. Fortunately he continued on into the shop and I was able to bundle everything back into the dustbin bag, take it outside and throw it into one of the large bins that stood in the yard.

When I came back, feeling slightly guilty, Jean was there filling the kettle. I told her what I'd done, and she said, "Best place for it. I wish people would stop treating us as a dumping ground for their junk."

"Why on earth is he photographing all those locks and things?" I asked.

"Oh, something to do with the maintenance of the premises — I haven't the faintest idea what that is all about." She switched off the kettle. "Do you want a coffee? I'm just making one for his lordship."

"No, thanks," I said regretfully. "I've only just got here. I'd better go and help Wendy."

I'd really got into the way of going to the shop and felt almost sorry that Monica would be coming back quite soon.

"I thought I might volunteer to help on a regular basis," I said to Rosemary. "I'm quite enjoying it."

"No way," Rosemary said vehemently.

"Think of having to put up with Norma and horrible Desmond forever more! Anyway, your volunteering has been a bit of a hindrance you must admit — we haven't had a day out for ages."

Michael was equally emphatic. "You'd hate it after a bit — you know you would. Day after day. Anyway, you've got quite enough on already — Brunswick Lodge and the Hospital Friends and all the other stuff."

I knew they were right, but still, I was quite pleased to get a phone call from Monica saying that she wouldn't be back for several weeks more.

"They've found dry rot in the new house," she said. "Would you believe it — after they had a survey and everything? I said to Julie, 'I hope you're going to sue that surveyor, with all the upset he's caused!' Anyway, they've had to make arrangements to stay on in their old house while it's being fixed — well, you can imagine how awkward that was. Fortunately the people they'd sold it to didn't want to move in straightaway — *he* had to go abroad for his job for a couple of months and she couldn't move on her own — wasn't that lucky. So you see, Sheila, I couldn't possibly leave them in the lurch now, especially with little Daniel still so delicate. I'm sure you understand. . . ."

I assured her that everything was fine and I'd be happy to fill in for her for a while longer.

"How are you getting on with Desmond?" she asked. "He can be a bit difficult. And Norma, too. But I'm sure you've been coping beautifully."

I told her that I was enjoying working at the shop.

"Well, they're a nice crowd, by and large. I was sure you'd get on all right with them. I must go. I can hear Daniel crying and I don't want to disturb Julie. She's having a little lie-down, poor girl — a lot of broken nights. . . . Thanks so much."

So that was that.

To pacify Rosemary I said we'd visit a stately home, one quite a long way off in Devon so it would be a whole day's outing.

"If we leave nice and early," I said, "we can have a good look round before we have lunch. It's a National Trust property, so there's bound to be a food place there, and then you can be back in time to get Jack's supper and I won't have to leave the animals for too long."

It was a lovely early summer day, sunny but not too hot, and the hedgerows were decorated with campions, foxgloves and the

39

first dog roses.

" 'Unkempt about those hedges blows / An English, unofficial rose,' " I quoted to Rosemary, as I do every year, merely, I suppose, for the pleasure of saying it.

She smiled. "It is all rather perfect, isn't it. Now, isn't this better than being shut up in that stuffy shop surrounded by the detritus of a hundred homes?"

"It's not as bad as that," I protested. "But you're right. It is nice to get out for a bit."

The stately home was very fine and full of beautiful objects and interesting furnishings, but I always find it sad and unsatisfactory when such a place is uninhabited and turned into a sort of museum. There's such a different atmosphere when the family's still in occupation. What Rosemary and I most enjoy are the personal possessions — the modern novel, spectacles beside it, left casually on a Sheraton table; the photographs (family, not royalty and nobility); a half-finished piece of embroidery laid down on a chair; the dog basket (with scruffy blanket and rubber bone) lying cozily beside the ornate marble fireplace — reminders that these grand houses were originally meant for people to live in.

Because we were quite early, there weren't many other visitors there, and we were able to make our way comfortably through the succession of rooms. In general we don't buy a guidebook, which I think makes you plod round conscientiously examining objects you are supposed to admire. We both belong to what Rosemary calls the Darting About School, moving around erratically as different things catch our eye. We may miss some of the more important objects, but we agree that it's much better (and more fun) to get the feel of the place.

"Goodness, what a disagreeable man!" Rosemary said, standing in front of a full-length portrait of an eighteenth-century gentleman, the elegance of whose silver-trimmed velvet coat, satin breeches and silver buckled shoes did little to mitigate the unpleasantness of his contemptuous gaze.

"Perfectly horrid," I agreed. "Actually, he has a look of Desmond — the way he is looking down his nose in that particularly sneering way. I wonder if his wife was anything like Wendy?"

"That's her," Rosemary said, moving to the adjacent portrait of a young, round-faced woman with two small children standing beside a large dog in the foreground. "Poor soul," Rosemary said, looking at the plaque at the side of the picture. "She died young — only twenty-two. In childbirth, I suppose."

I joined her in front of the picture. The round face looked as if it was made for laughing, but the expression was wistful and the eyes were sad. She seemed constricted not only by the stiff formality of her elaborate dress but by something more intangible. It was not difficult to imagine a melancholy life — even the children (boys, young enough to be still in petticoats) stood apart from her, more attached to their dog than their mother.

"I wonder if he married again?" Rosemary said.

"Poor little thing," I said. "I suppose that one was an arranged marriage — land or something — so I expect he did."

We stood for a moment looking at the two portraits.

"We're probably quite wrong," Rosemary said, "carried away by the resemblance to Desmond. For all we know, he was madly in love with her and pined away and died himself. Perhaps we ought to buy a book and see what it says about him."

"But it won't," I said. "They never do tell you the things you really want to know. Anyway, it's almost lunchtime. Shall we go and get something to eat before it's too crowded?"

There weren't many people in the café. We chose our food at the counter — National Trust quiche (which never seems to vary from one stately home to another) with the obligatory salad leaves, chocolate gateau for me, a coffee one for Rosemary, and sparkling water because Rosemary was driving — and looked around for a suitable table. Rosemary started off towards the back of the room, but I motioned her to move towards the window. I'd seen Wendy at the farthest end of the room in earnest conversation with her son, John.

We put our food on the table, and Rosemary complained, as she always does, that there's never anywhere to put your empty tray.

"Fancy seeing them," I said. "I wonder how they got here. I know Wendy doesn't drive and I'm sure John hasn't got a car."

"I expect they came by bus," Rosemary said. "It's not that far to walk up from the main road. Did you see any salad dressing on the counter? Oh well, I suppose I can do without."

"But it is rather odd," I persisted.

"I don't see why they shouldn't be having a day out, the same as us."

"Somehow I don't connect Wendy with days out," I said. "And they seem very deep

43

in a serious conversation — they don't look as if they're *enjoying* themselves. Perhaps this is the only way they can get to talk to each other without Desmond overhearing what they're saying."

"It seems a bit extreme. No, I think it's just a little treat, and goodness knows they'd certainly need one now and again, living in that household. This pastry isn't very nice. How's yours?"

"It's a bit hard." I glanced over towards them. "Perhaps it's something special that they can't risk him knowing about."

"It seems a long way to come for that."

"Maybe Wendy just wanted to give him a nice day out, before he goes back to college. Oh, they're leaving now."

As they moved towards the door, Wendy suddenly saw us. For a moment she looked shocked and surprised. Then she gave us a little nervous smile and a sort of half wave in recognition, but made no attempt to come over and speak to us.

The next time I saw Wendy in the shop, I didn't say anything about our having seen her and she didn't refer to it. I thought she looked even more anxious than usual and said to Jean, "Wendy looks especially worried today. Is anything wrong?"

44

Jean stopped putting clothes hangers on a rack and said, "Not that I know of. Just his lordship being more difficult than usual, I expect. It's always worse when John is at home." She pushed the rack nearer the wall. "I wish to goodness Norma didn't insist on having these large racks over here where we all keep tripping over the feet — I mean, look at the way they stick out. I've told her about it several times, but she never listens to anything she doesn't want to hear. Oh well. When someone falls over them and breaks something, she'll have the health and safety people onto her — and see how she likes that!"

Jean never missed an opportunity to criticize Norma. It was one of the games she enjoyed playing, finding small, irritating niggles to confront her with. Usually Norma rose above it, smiling loftily as if Jean's opinion wasn't really worth having. Just occasionally some shaft would go home, and then she gave Jean what I'm sure she thought of as One of her Setdowns, which, although it didn't subdue Jean, doubtless gave Norma some sort of satisfaction.

"Do you want to have a go at a couple of these dresses?" Jean asked. "If you feel like tackling the steamer."

"I don't know," I said nervously, looking

at the poster on the wall giving a blow-by-blow description of how *not* to use it, and dire warnings about how dangerous it was. "It all looks a bit complicated. Norma says . . ."

"Oh, you don't want to listen to her. She always tries to make out that she's the only one who can manage anything — look how she is about the till, and you're fine with that now."

"Well, if you think it's OK."

She filled the apparatus with cold water and told me (in simpler terms than the warning poster) how to use it. "You just have to move it up and down on the garment — you see, like this. I'm supposed to stay with you while you use it, but I'm sure you can manage. The worst damage you can do to yourself is get arm ache from holding the wretched thing up!"

I eventually managed to take the steamer in my stride (Jean was right about the arm ache). It was quite satisfying to see a garment freshen up under the steamer's influence, though I never got over the sense of irritation whenever Norma decided to stand over me to see that I did it properly. What I did prefer doing was pricing the garments, though the list we had as a guide was obviously intended for somewhere much grander and more fashionable than Taviscombe, since it included names like Dior and Stella McCartney.

I was attempting to price some of the clothes that Norma had got from one of her richer contacts ("I find that the personal touch always produces results"). I wasn't usually allowed to do this, Norma wishing to keep this little treat for herself, but she'd been called away by Desmond for a discussion about some important policy decision (so she said) and reluctantly allowed me to take over. Since I felt as capable as she was to read the labels in the garments, I was quite enjoying the job. There were certainly some rather desirable things, and I was just wondering if I might use my ten percent discount to buy a really elegant blouse (Jaeger) when Margaret came in. I was surprised to see her, since people don't often come in on the days they're off duty.

"Hello," I said. "Fancy seeing you here!"

She looked a little disconcerted. "Oh, Desmond asked me to come in."

"Oh?"

"He didn't say why."

Desmond came into the storeroom then and seemed annoyed to find me there.

"Mrs. Malory" (he never used Christian names), "perhaps you would be good

47

enough to find something useful to do in the shop. I would like to have a word with Miss Curtis." He held open the door and then closed it firmly behind me.

Jean and Wendy were checking through some DVDs before putting them on the shelves. You have to do that to make sure they're not pirated — something I'd never have thought of. Norma was rearranging items of jewelry in the case at the counter. She looked very upset about something, but I suppose a "discussion" with Desmond might upset anyone.

"Is there anything special you want me to do?" I asked.

"What?"

I repeated the question.

"Oh, you could take down those ornaments — carefully — and dust the shelves."

Her mind was obviously elsewhere, and she kept looking at the closed door of the storeroom. I removed the ornaments (carefully), dusted the shelves (which didn't need dusting) and replaced the objects. Fortunately a couple of people came in and needed help so that when Desmond came back into the shop, I was usefully employed. He nodded to Norma and went away. After a little while Margaret came out of the storeroom. She didn't speak to any of us as she went out, but I caught a glimpse of her face and it looked as though she'd been crying.

CHAPTER FOUR

The concerts at Brunswick Lodge are always pleasant occasions. Nothing elaborate, just piano recitals and the occasional string quartet. They are organized by the grandly titled arts committee. My friend Anthea, who more or less runs Brunswick Lodge, has been locked into a long-standing feud with Julia Morrison, who is the arts committee chairman, so she ostentatiously avoids all their activities. Unfortunately she didn't learn, until it was too late, that Julia was moving to Canada to live with her married daughter, and when she *did* find out, Norma had (by a judicious mixture of bribery, blackmail and force of personality) been elected chairman in her place. Such are the Byzantine politics of Brunswick Lodge, and a brand-new feud is now, inevitably, in full force.

I thought of this when I found myself sitting next to Norma's husband, Marcus, at a recital the following weekend. I'd met him several times before at various Brunswick Lodge events, and I sometimes saw him when he was stewarding or helping at bring-and-buy sales (presumably press-ganged by Norma). He also came into the shop occasionally to bring or collect various items, was ordered about peremptorily and never thanked for his efforts. "You can't even feel sorry for him," Jean said. "He's just *so* feeble!" But I suppose, if you dote on someone (as he obviously dotes on Norma), then you're quite happy to be treated like that by the object of your devotion. Certainly he always seemed quite cheerful — jolly, even.

"Hello, Sheila," he greeted me. "Quite a good turnout. I'm so glad — Norma's had to work very hard to get this chap. He's reckoned to be one of the finest exponents of Liszt in the country."

"How splendid," I said. "And how clever of Norma to persuade him."

"Of course, we can't afford his usual fee, but Norma explained it was for charity and such a good cause."

"I'm sure Norma was very persuasive." He looked pleased, so I went on. "I can't think how she manages to fit in so many things — though, of course, she's so very

51

well organized."

He positively beamed with pleasure at this. "Of course, you see her at work in the charity shop — Norma often speaks of you."

I didn't pursue that remark since I didn't think Norma went in much for praise of her fellow workers. Just then Norma herself appeared and, giving me a cursory nod, addressed herself to Marcus.

"Don't forget, I need you to stack the chairs and put them away afterwards. James should be doing it, but he's got to drive this man to catch his train. Oh yes, and make sure you lock the storeroom door after you've put the chairs away and bring me the key." She caught sight of a new arrival. "Oh, there's Councilor Martin — I need to speak to him about the rubbish collection. The men left several bags of rubbish the gardening committee put out last week, after I'd specifically arranged for them to be collected. Now remember, do the chairs *straight*away after the recital because I need to have everything locked up before ten forty-five."

I'd been discreetly perusing my program while this was going on, not wishing to embarrass poor Marcus by witnessing this interchange. But he seemed perfectly unconcerned and said, "Isn't it marvelous the way she thinks of absolutely everything!"

Fortunately the pianist now made his appearance, and I was spared the need to reply.

Marcus was in the storeroom the following week, moving boxes of books to go for disposal. He greeted me cheerfully. "Norma asked me to pop in to shift this lot — they're a bit heavy for you ladies, even with the trolley."

Just then Desmond came in. He disapproved of non–staff members being on the premises — the dreaded health and safety thing and something called employers' liability, terms he made great play with. I felt he was about to say something unpleasant to Marcus, so I hastily went into the shop. Marcus didn't reappear, and I assumed he'd gone out the back way, into the alley. After quite a while Desmond came out, and he and Norma had a low-toned conversation at the back of the shop that went on for some time and appeared to please neither of them.

After he'd gone I went back into the storeroom where Jean was struggling to open a large cardboard box.

"Greeting cards," she said to my inquiry. "It's the only thing we buy in." She fumbled ineffectually at the fastening. "This wretched tape's impossible; these scissors are useless. I'll have to get a knife out of the kitchen."

She disappeared into the little cubbyhole where the kettle was kept along with a small fridge where people could leave their sandwiches for lunch and a cabinet with shelves for cups and plates and a drawer for cutlery.

"Let's see if this will do it," she said, brandishing a large kitchen knife and attacking the recalcitrant tape with vigor.

"Don't let Desmond see you with that," I said. "Think of the health and safety!"

"Bother Desmond! Anyway, it's done it now. There." She went on unpacking some cards, and pushing a pile of garments to one side, she spread them out on the table. "They're rather nice. Tasteful. I like this one of a bluebell wood and this one of the roses — I might as well get a couple while I think of it. This is a terrible month for birthdays."

"They are rather nice," I said. "I'll get that one with the spaniel for Thea. She's got a birthday soon, and this is just like their dog Truffy. How much are they?"

"One pound twenty-five — but don't forget your ten percent discount!"

Desmond came back just after lunch and

really surpassed himself. It was a slack afternoon, and he gathered us all together in the storeroom and gave us a lecture on how useless we all were about selling and how we weren't "making sales" and how our turnover was down on last year and how compared with the other charity shops in the town (he'd got comparative figures, which he read out with great relish) we were way behind and how this was a commercial enterprise and not a social gathering or a mothers' meeting where ladies stand about chatting. . . . After a while I gave up listening and amused myself by looking at the faces of the others. Predictably Wendy was listening intently — no doubt she'd be questioned about his "little talk" when she got home. Jean appeared to be intent on examining her colorless nail varnish, picking at a bit that was chipped and yawning from time to time. Norma was absolutely bursting with fury — you could see what a tremendous effort she was making not to say anything. When Desmond finally finished and went away, saying that he'd be back to go to the bank with the takings, Norma, who was quite red in the face, gathered up her coat, said she had a headache and was going home, and swept out of the shop.

"Well!" Jean said. "What a carry-on!"

Wendy looked very distressed. "Oh dear, poor Norma — I'm sure Desmond didn't mean anyone to take it personally. It's just that he's so anxious that the shop will do well. . . ." Her voice trailed away.

Seeing how miserable she looked, I said, "I'm going to put the kettle on. I'm sure we'll all be much more efficient when we've had a cup of tea."

Jean gave a snort of laughter and went back into the shop.

The rest of the afternoon passed peacefully. We made a few sales, which I hoped might please Desmond. What with one thing and another I was quite late leaving, and I was on the point of going home when he came in to collect the takings. He seemed annoyed when he heard about Norma, although Wendy tried to say tactfully that she'd had a headache all day.

"It's extremely tiresome," he said. "I was held up at a meeting that went on too long, so now it's too late for the bank."

Since he never allowed Norma to see to the takings herself, I didn't see why his being late for the bank was her fault. Still, Desmond never really required any sort of logic when it came to finding someone to blame.

"Well, I'm off," Jean said. And with a cheery wave to me and to Wendy, but not to Desmond, she left.

"Are you coming back now?" Wendy approached her husband tentatively.

He looked up from the papers he'd taken out of his briefcase. "No," he said brusquely. "I shall be some time — I have things to do here. I don't know when I'll be back. Don't wait supper. You can get me something when I get in. Oh, and tell John I want to speak to him when I come in."

We both got our coats and handbags and Wendy collected the numerous small parcels she always seemed to be burdened with. Desmond unlocked the shop door to let us out. As I looked back, I saw that he'd gone into the storeroom again and I wondered what were the "things" he had to do — more targets for us, no doubt.

"I do hope Norma wasn't too upset," Wendy said. "Like I said, Desmond doesn't mean these things personally. Oh I know he put things — well, you know, a little strongly — but that's just his way. . . ." Her voice trailed off, and I wondered how often she'd tried to placate people he had offended. She looked very weary and, on an impulse, I said, "Can I give you a lift home? You seem to have so much to carry."

"Oh no, it's all right. I can get the bus."

"Come on," I urged her. "Look, it's starting to rain, and here's the car. Hop in." I opened the doors. "Put your parcel on the backseat."

"Well, that is very kind. Thank you so much. I'm afraid I've missed my usual bus and the next one will be quite a while. . . ."

The Barlows lived on the outskirts of town, and we didn't talk much on the way. Wendy looked exhausted, and I couldn't really think of anything to say. I pulled up outside the house — it was a large, modern house, set in a well-kept garden.

As she got out, Wendy said tentatively, "Would you like to come in for a drink or a cup of tea?"

I was quite taken aback by the invitation, the last thing I expected. But the opportunity to see inside the house was irresistible. "That would be lovely," I said, and followed her up the path. I held some of the parcels while she fumbled in her bag for the key, and we finally went inside. The hall was spacious with a handsome staircase, and I got the impression of highly polished parquet flooring everywhere. Wendy led me into the sitting room (more parquet with some expensive rugs). Although the room still held the late-afternoon sunshine (windows on both sides) and the furniture was modern in light wood, the general effect was cold and clinical. Apart from a formal arrangement of large flowers, there were no personal touches — no books, pictures or photographs — only a neat pile of copies of *Somerset Life* on a coffee table. It seemed unlikely that anyone actually lived in the room; in its way it looked like the modern upmarket equivalent of the old traditional front parlor.

"Do sit down," Wendy said, "and I'll get rid of these parcels. What would you like to drink?"

"Tea would be lovely," I said.

"Are you sure? We have sherry and gin and, and things. . . ."

"No, really, tea will be fine."

She looked faintly relieved, and I wondered if Desmond might have disapproved of her offering this hospitality. I sat down cautiously on the large sofa, trying not to lean back and disturb the carefully arranged cushions. From where I sat I could see, through one of the windows, the back garden, also large and well kept, but also impersonal, more like a park garden tended by a professional gardener; again no personal touches.

Wendy was away for quite a while, and I thought I heard voices and then the slamming of a door. She appeared soon after, bearing a tray with tea things and a plate of biscuits.

"Sorry I've been so long."

She looked rather upset, but she poured the tea and offered me a biscuit. "Do have one. It's a bourbon — I think that's your favorite."

I was touched that she'd noticed how I always chose the bourbon when there was a selection of biscuits at the shop.

"How sweet of you," I said. "I adore them." I took a biscuit and tried to make conversation. "Isn't this a pleasant room — lovely to have windows on both sides. It makes it so nice and light. My cottage has such tiny windows the sun hardly ever gets in, and I have to have the light on even in the summer!"

She smiled. "It must be nice to live in an old house. This was new when we moved into it. Desmond doesn't like old houses. He says they always need things doing to them."

"He's so right," I said. "I spend an absolute fortune on my thatched roof, the chimneys are in a state of collapse and, of course, there's the everlasting problem of

60

the septic tank!"

"But you wouldn't want to live anywhere else?"

"There are times, when yet another thing goes wrong, that all I want is to move into a little modern box — but no, you're right. I wouldn't be happy anywhere else."

"I always wanted to live in one of those cottages by the harbor," Wendy said, "where you can see the sea. But Desmond said they opened up right onto the street and there would be passersby all the time."

"I suppose so," I said. "But I do so agree about the sea. Whenever I feel a bit down or want to think about anything, I always go down and look at the sea. It's a sort of comfort — the waves, I suppose, and that expanse of water. It puts things in perspective somehow."

Wendy smiled. "My grandfather was in the Navy, so I suppose the sea is in my blood, as they say. But we lived in the Midlands, and it seemed so far away!"

"Did you have to move about a lot because of Desmond's job?"

"Yes, quite a lot. That's why I was so pleased when Desmond retired and we could settle in one place."

"What made you choose Taviscombe?"

"Oh, Desmond's cousin was vicar of St.

Mary's — the previous vicar, not this one — and he knew Desmond was a lay preacher; he had been for some years. So he said, Why didn't Desmond come to St. Mary's?"

"So you moved to Taviscombe. Were you pleased? Was it where you wanted to live?"

She hesitated. "Desmond was set on Taviscombe, and really, we've settled down here very nicely. There's so much here for Desmond to do — he likes that. And, of course there's the sea. . . ."

"Well," I said. "I suppose I should be getting back."

"Won't you have another cup of tea, or a biscuit?"

"No, thanks. I must be on my way. My animals have been in all day so I ought to go and let them out."

"Oh, do you have animals? What are they?"

"A dog — a Westie — and a very demanding Siamese cat."

"How lovely. I've always wanted a cat. But, of course, moving about as we did, Desmond said it wouldn't be fair."

"But you're settled down here."

"Well, it's too late now, I suppose . . ."

I got up and she came with me to the door. "Thank you so much," I said. "It's been really nice. You must come and see me — and the animals."

She smiled wistfully. "That would be lovely."

As I drove away, she was still standing at the door, watching me until I was out of sight.

"Poor little soul," I said to Rosemary when I told her all about it later. "I don't believe she's ever dared to invite anyone back — she only did it because she knew Desmond would be out for a long time."

"Oh, that man!" Rosemary said vehemently. "He's abominable. And how does she stand it? In this day and age you wouldn't credit it."

"I suppose there'll always be people like Desmond bullying people like Wendy; it's human nature and there's nothing anyone can do about it."

"How can that son of hers stand by and let it happen?"

"He's even more frightened of Desmond than she is."

"Well, I've no patience with either of them. Why hasn't she left him ages ago?"

"I don't imagine she has anywhere else to go and probably no money."

"She could get a job."

"Not easy at her age."

"The son could."

"He's at university — she wouldn't want him to give that up. No, I'm afraid there's no solution — anyway, I suppose she's used to it by now."

"Well, she shouldn't have to be," Rosemary said. "It's not fair."

I smiled. "Whoever said that life was fair?" I replied.

CHAPTER FIVE

The next morning, because the animals were more cooperative than usual, I was down at the charity shop nice and early. The shop door was still locked, of course, so I went round to the alley at the back. I stopped short in surprise — there was a policeman standing by the door to the shop's backyard, and the entrance was cordoned off by police tape. The constable came towards me and said, "Sorry. I'm afraid you can't come in."

"But I work in the shop," I said.

"I'm sorry — there's been an incident."

"An incident?"

He seemed disinclined to elaborate further, and I was about to protest when the door opened and Inspector Morris came out. I've known Bob Morris since he was a little boy who used to come and help his father when he looked after my garden.

"Bob," I said, "what's going on?"

He nodded at the constable, who went back into the yard. "I'm afraid it's serious, Mrs. Malory." He thought for a moment and then he said, "I believe you've been helping out here?"

"Yes. I've been filling in for someone who's away."

"Right. Well, I'm afraid we are investigating the death of Mr. Desmond Barlow."

"Dead? Investigating? You mean someone killed him?"

He paused again. "I wonder if you could help me. We've had to ask Mrs. Barlow to come in and identify her husband and, obviously, she's very upset. I wonder if you could very kindly take her home?"

"Oh, poor Wendy! Of course I will. She must be devastated."

"That would be a great help — more comfortable for her to have someone she knows."

He went back into the yard. After a few minutes, Wendy came out supported by a policewoman. I went over and put my arm round her shoulders.

"I'm so sorry," I said. "Such a terrible thing to have happened. Let's get you home."

Again in the car, like last time, neither of us spoke. There seemed nothing I could usefully say, and Wendy seemed stunned by what had happened. There were no tears. She sat beside me, her hands tightly locked together, her face blank and her eyes fixed unseeing on the road ahead. At the house she gave me her keys, and I opened the door and we went inside. She stood silently in the hall, as if waiting to be told what to do next.

"Shall we go into the kitchen," I suggested, "and I'll make us a cup of tea."

She led the way down a passage into a kitchen that was as neat and impersonal as the rest of the house. It was a large kitchen with a sort of dining area with a table and four chairs. I pulled out one of the chairs for her and she sat down obediently. I filled the kettle and found the tea, milk and cups and saucers while she watched me as though she was a stranger in a strange house. When I had made the tea, she drank some of it mechanically, still saying nothing. Then she spoke, quietly and without any sort of emotion.

"Someone killed Desmond — with a knife, they said. They'd put a sheet over him, but they uncovered his face." She drank some more of her tea. "He looked the same, just surprised." She looked directly at me for the first time. "But it's true

— he is dead."

I moved over and took her hand. "Yes, it is true. I'm so sorry, Wendy. It's horrible for you."

She began to cry. Not sobbing, just tears rolling unchecked down her face. I put my arm round her. "Try to let go," I said. "Don't hold it in — you'll feel better if you let it out."

She brushed away the tears and shook her head. "No, really, I'm all right." She drank some more tea, and I went back and sat down opposite her.

"Is there anyone I can call?"

She shook her head again.

"What about John? Where is he? Does he know?"

"He's not here — he went back to college yesterday."

"Oh, I didn't think term had started yet."

"He had things to do."

"Of course." There was a pause, and then I said, "Will you get in touch with him? I'm sure he'd want to be with you at a time like this."

"No, no. He mustn't come back — he's got things to do and I'm — I'm all right." She attempted a smile. "It's just that it's been a dreadful shock."

"Of course." Another pause. "Will you

68

ring him? To tell him what's happened."

She became agitated. "No — I can't — I don't know what to say. . . ."

"Would you like me to tell him? If you could give me his mobile number."

"Yes. Yes, that would be best. Just tell him what's happened. I can't. . . ."

She got up suddenly and searched in her handbag and produced a piece of paper with a mobile number on it. "I always carry it with me — John says I must — just in case. The phone — the phone's in the hall."

I went out into the hall, and she made no attempt to follow me but sat down again at the kitchen table.

I rang the number. There was quite a pause before a voice said cautiously, "Who is it?"

"Is that John Barlow?"

"Who is it?" he repeated.

"My name's Sheila Malory. I'm a friend of your mother's. We work together in the charity shop."

"What's happened? Is she all right? What's happened?" His voice rose.

"No, your mother's fine. It's about your father."

"Oh."

"I'm afraid it's your father — I'm so sorry to have to tell you. He's dead."

69

"Dead? What happened, was it an accident?"

"No — look, there's no easy way to say this — he's been killed."

"Killed?"

"Murdered."

There was a long pause. Then he said, "My mother — how is she?"

"Very upset."

"What has she said?" His voice rose again.

"Not a lot — I think she's still in shock. The police needed her to identify the body — he was killed at the shop. It must have been terrible for her. I brought her home. If you like I can stay with her until you get here."

"It may be difficult — right away, that is. . . ."

"Look," I said. "Your mother asked me to break the news to you — I think she found it difficult — but I do think you should have a word with her now. I'll go and get her for you." I put down the phone before he could reply and went back into the kitchen.

"Wendy," I said. "John would like to have word with you."

She shook her head.

"I think you should," I went on. "He's obviously worried about you. Come along."

I went with her into the hall and watched

her pick up the phone. Then I went back into the kitchen and poured myself another cup of tea. After quite a short time she came back and sat down again.

"Is he coming home?" I asked.

"No, I told him not to."

"But surely . . ."

"He has things to do." She was quite agitated and twisted her hands together. "He has to see people about his course — it's important."

"I'm sure they'd understand, given the circumstances."

"It's all right — I'm all right."

"Are you sure? What can I do?"

"No, it's very kind of you — you've been so kind, but I'm all right."

"Can I get you some lunch or anything?"

"I don't feel much like eating — but I'll have some soup or a boiled egg later. No, really, I'm all right. Thank you for everything."

She got to her feet, and I was obliged to do the same.

"Well, if you're sure. . . . Well, look, I'll leave my phone number and just ring — anytime — if there's anything I can do."

I found a bit of paper in my handbag, scribbled the number on it and left it on the table. Wendy went into the hall and opened the front door. I stood for a moment in the doorway.

"I don't like leaving you all alone like this," I said. "Are you sure there's nothing I can do?"

"No, thank you very much. I'm all right. I'm quite all right."

I went out to the car and, like the last time, when I looked back she was standing at the door watching me go.

"Poor soul," Rosemary said when I told her. "She must be completely lost."

"Yes," I said. "*Lost.* That's the exact word. Lost and bewildered. I do wish John would come home — I really can't understand it; they've always seemed so close. I know she told him not to, but really . . ."

"From what you've told me, he sounds as flaky as she is."

"Weak, certainly. But not surprising, given what Desmond was like."

"It's a bit odd," Rosemary went on. "If Desmond was killed last night, then why wasn't she worried when he didn't come home? Did she phone the shop?"

"Goodness knows. He did say, when we were leaving, that he'd be late home, so perhaps she'd gone to bed. They seem to have found the body quite early this morning."

"How? Who actually found him?"

"I don't know. I suppose it must have been Norma — she's always the first one there. It must have been a dreadful shock for her. Anyway," I said, "I don't suppose anyone is going to tell us anything about it today."

But I was wrong. Late in the afternoon Bob Morris arrived.

"Sorry to bother you, Mrs. Malory. But as you work at the shop, I do need to ask you a few questions, if you wouldn't mind."

"Of course, come in." I led the way into the kitchen. "I was just about to have some tea. Will you join me?"

"That would be nice." He sat down and looked around him. "It doesn't seem so long ago that I was here with Dad. I see you've still got that Christmas cactus — it's grown a bit since then."

"I know — I keep repotting it and I've divided it a couple of times. There's a cutting there on the windowsill, if you'd like it — or would that be bribing the police? Though, since it was your father who gave it to me in the first place, I suppose it would be all right."

He smiled. "That would be very kind. Dad would like to see it. He's still interested though he doesn't manage to get outside at all now."

I made the tea and cut him a slice of chocolate cake ("It used to be your favorite"), aware that I was chattering away because I somehow didn't want to have to talk about the shop and, especially, about Wendy.

He ate the cake and then said, "How was Mrs. Barlow?"

"Not good — she was still in shock, I suppose. She didn't say much and, really, I didn't feel I could either. I offered to stay, but she wouldn't let me."

"She has a son, hasn't she?"

"Yes, he's away at university. I expect he'll come back soon to be with her."

I cut him another slice of cake and one for myself. "Who found him?" I asked. "Mr. Barlow, I mean."

"It was early this morning — well, about six o'clock. One of the constables was on patrol. As he went along that alley at the back he saw the yard gate was open and there was a light on. When he went to investigate, he found the back door of the shop open as well. Mr. Barlow was in the back room."

"You don't know when he died?"

"We haven't had the forensic report yet,

but as far as I could judge, he must have been dead for some hours. Do you have any idea what he was doing in the shop yesterday evening?"

"He often stayed on after the shop was shut, looking at the stock, checking the books — that sort of thing. He was very — very hands on, as they say."

"I see."

"Actually, as we were leaving — I was giving Wendy a lift home — he did say to her that he would be late home."

He nodded. "I see," he said again.

Looking at him, a small, neat, self-contained man, I remembered an eleven-year-old, small, neat, self-contained boy sitting quietly and patiently at the same table, eating his cake and listening with apparent interest as his father and I discussed early flowering clematis and overwintering dahlias. I could see how that quiet manner and patient listening would be invaluable in his present career.

"There are a couple of things about the shop," he said. "I had hoped to ask Mrs. Stanley, but apparently she's not well."

Norma's migraines, I thought. Well, there was every reason for her to have a migraine now.

"It's about the money," Bob continued.

"Oh yes. Well, Desmond usually came in in the afternoon and bagged up the cash in the till and took it to the bank. No one else was allowed to do it. So if he couldn't, then the money was taken out of the till and put away in a safe place at the back of the shop. You always had to leave the till open so that anyone looking in would see that it was empty."

"Did he go to the bank yesterday?"

"No, he arrived too late."

"And do you know where the safe place was?" he asked.

"I'm sorry. I don't. I think only Norma knew — or possibly Jean Lucas; she's been there longest."

"That would explain why the till was empty." He paused as if to file away that information before he went on to the next question. "The other thing is — I saw there was a sort of kitchen out at the back. Were any knives kept there?"

"Knives? Well, yes, there are several." I stopped suddenly and looked at him. "Was that what was used to kill him?"

He looked at me inquiringly.

"Wendy said he'd been stabbed," I said.

"We don't know what the weapon was — it had been taken away — but it did occur to me that if there was one on the premises . . ."

"Jean used one from the kitchen to open a package yesterday afternoon. It was quite a large one — we used it to open packages, like I said. I don't think she put it back so it would have been just lying there."

"I see. Well, that's been very helpful."

"If there's anything else you want know. . . ."

"I may take you up on that, seeing as how you know the setup, so to speak."

He got up, and I went over and fetched the Christmas cactus.

"Hang on a moment," I said. "I'll put it in a bag for you. You won't want to take it into the station like that."

He smiled. "No, that's all right. They're used to me turning up with plants of all sorts. Dad will be really pleased to see this — it's quite an unusual variety."

When he'd gone and I was preparing vegetables for supper, I went over in my mind what Desmond had actually said to Wendy as we were leaving. "Don't wait supper. You can get me something when I get in." That didn't sound as if he intended to be very late — even Desmond would hardly expect Wendy to get up and make supper for him if she'd gone to bed. And there was something else — he'd said he wanted to speak to John when he got home. So John would have been expecting him. Why weren't either of them concerned when Desmond hadn't come back home when they expected him? I remembered the voices I'd heard — one of them must have been John. So when *did* he go back to university? And why was Wendy so anxious that John shouldn't return?

The knife slipped as I was chopping the last bit of an onion and I cut my finger. As I sprayed it with iodine and put a plaster on, I reflected that it was *not* a good idea to try to assemble my thoughts on a murder when I had a knife in my hand.

Chapter Six

It was several days before we were able to go back into the shop. I had a phone call in the morning from Norma (rather subdued, not surprising in the circumstances) saying that she hoped to open up the next day but she wanted us all, the complete staff, to come in after lunch that day for a short meeting. She added that we should use the shop entrance — the door would be locked, but if we rang the bell she would open it.

I think we were all glad not to have to use the back entrance, and I noticed that the door between the shop and the back room was firmly shut. We greeted each other with a kind of muted sympathy, as people do after a funeral.

"Thank you all for coming," Norma said. "Wendy won't be with us, of course. I thought we might all contribute for some flowers to be sent to her with our good wishes." There was a murmur of approval.

"Meanwhile, the police have said that we can open the shop again tomorrow, and" — she paused, perhaps for effect — "I'm sure that's what Desmond would have wanted us to do."

There was another murmur of agreement, though I heard Jean mutter something about sales figures. "I believe," Norma went on, "the police have spoken to some of you about what happened on that day, and I'm sure we all want to do everything we can to assist them." Another murmur. "Now, I don't know if there are any questions?"

"There is one thing," I said. "Inspector Morris was asking about the day's takings, since Desmond hadn't arrived in time to take them to the bank. Were they put away safely as they usually are?"

Norma looked annoyed at my question. "As it happens, they weren't. I would normally have done so but, you may remember I — I had to leave a little early. I naturally assumed Desmond would do so — he was, as you know, most meticulous about such things."

"But he didn't?" I asked.

"Apparently not," Norma said shortly. "No doubt he intended to do so before he left, but, of course . . ."

"So the money is missing?"

"It would seem so."

The murmuring this time was quite different.

"You mean somebody *stole* it?" Margaret asked.

"That appears to be the case."

"But if Desmond was here —" Margaret began, then stopped suddenly.

"What Margaret was trying to say," Jean said in her forthright way, "is that someone must have come in and seen Desmond's dead body but went right on into the shop and took the money out of the till."

"And didn't call the police?" Margaret asked, her voice trembling a little.

"Not likely, is it," Jean said, "if they'd just robbed the shop?" A series of exclamations of surprise and horror. "I know — it doesn't bear thinking about it, even if he was actually dead. Though I suppose he might not have died instantly."

"Yes, well," Norma said hastily. "I am sure the police have all that in hand. The other thing I wanted to say to you all is that I'm afraid — human nature being what it is — we may have some customers who will be here not to buy anything, but prompted by curiosity. I'm sure I needn't tell you that it would be most improper for any of us to discuss the situation in any way, and I'm sure that none of you would ever do so."

"So who's in charge now?" Jean asked.

Norma regarded her coldly. "I have been asked to take over as manager. I am sure we'll all pull together as a team, especially in these difficult times."

Jean looked as if she was going to say something, but Norma went on. "I've put this bowl on the counter for any contribution you may want to make for poor Wendy's flowers, and I've written a card sending her our best wishes."

"Could we all sign the card?" Dorothy asked tentatively. "I mean, if we're all contributing."

"Yes, of course," Norma said smoothly. "I'll leave it on the counter by the bowl." She turned and went into the back room.

We all watched her in silence, as though she was entering another world. Then a buzz of conversation broke out.

"I don't see why she should be manager," Margaret said. "Jean's been here much longer."

"That's right," Dorothy agreed. "So have you, and I have, too, though I wouldn't ever want to be manager. Too much responsibility!"

"And paperwork," Jean said. "Not to mention having to come in every day. No, I wouldn't want to do it either, but I must say I do resent the way she swans in here and takes over everything."

I went over to the counter and put some money in the bowl, and the others followed suit.

Margaret picked up the card. "She's just taken one of our cards — the 'Deepest Sympathy' one — off the rack. I hope she put the money in the till."

This was felt to be a remark too far. We all signed the card, and Jean put it in the envelope.

After a few minutes Norma came back into the shop and people began to disperse. As I was about to leave, Norma called me back.

"As you're not in tomorrow, Sheila, I thought it might be a nice gesture if you would get the flowers and take them personally to Wendy."

"Yes, of course."

Norma emptied the money in the bowl into a large envelope, added a five-pound note, and handed it to me. "Thank you so much. And now I must get on — there's a great deal to do before we open tomorrow."

The next morning I went to get the flowers. A nice big colorful bunch, not funeral flowers like lilies or chrysanthemums. I wondered if I should phone first, but I thought it might be easier for Wendy if I simply turned up on the doorstep and handed in the flowers. Then she could invite me in or not, depending on how she felt. As it turned out she seemed glad to see me.

"Sheila, how kind. Do come in." She led the way into the sitting room. I handed her the flowers and the card.

"We all wanted you to know that we're thinking of you," I said inadequately.

She held the flowers awkwardly, as if she didn't know what to do with them, and fumbled with the card. "How kind," she repeated. She put the flowers down on the table and read the card. " 'Deepest Sympathy' — how very kind of everyone. I'll just go and put the flowers in water. Do sit down."

I turned to sit down on the unyielding sofa and, to my surprise, I found it occupied by a large tabby cat.

"Oh, that's Tiger," Wendy said. "He's a stray, poor thing. He's been hanging around here for ages. Desmond always made me drive him away, but he lives here now." She picked up the flowers and went out of the room.

I sat down beside the cat, who regarded

me impassively. "Well, Tiger," I said. "Fancy that!"

As I stroked him, I looked round the room. It was subtly different. The cushions, for instance, were scattered about anyhow. There were magazines, books and newspapers laid down carelessly. And on the mantelpiece there was an unframed snapshot of a boy (presumably John) with Wendy, laughing on a beach in the sunshine.

Wendy came back into the room with a tray. "I hope you have time to stay for coffee," she said. "It's only instant, I'm afraid. Desmond always liked what he called proper coffee, but it takes forever to make and I really can't tell the difference." She handed me a cup and offered some biscuits. "Bourbons — you see, I did remember."

"How are you?" I asked. "Has John come back?"

"No, not yet."

"But he'll be back for the funeral?"

"Oh yes. But that won't be for ages yet because of the inquest — that nice police inspector explained all about it."

"Of course. It must be a difficult time for you."

"Sheila, can I ask you something?"

"Yes, of course," I said, expecting some question about funeral arrangements.

"You know about animals, don't you? Do you think I ought to take Tiger to the vet for injections and things? I mean, he's a stray, and I don't know if he's had them."

"Well, yes," I replied, disconcerted.

"I mean, he's been wandering about the streets, poor little thing. Goodness knows what he might have picked up. You should have seen him when he first turned up — so thin! I used to buy tins and put food out for him, down at the bottom of the garden, behind that big escallonia, where you couldn't see him from the house. Desmond didn't know, did he, Tiger?" Tiger narrowed his eyes and blinked at her. She smiled. "He understands every word I say! So you think I should take him to the vet?"

"Certainly. He may need to be de-flead, if nothing else," I said.

"Well, I'll have to get a cat basket. And —" She broke off. "And I can take him in the car!" I looked at her questioningly. "Desmond would never let me use the car," she said, "except when he needed me to drive him somewhere."

"That would certainly be easier," I said. I paused for a moment. "How are you managing — in general, I mean?"

"Oh, I'm *fine.*" This time the word had a cheerful sound, not like on my previous visit. This time she sounded as if she really meant it. "No, actually, I'm managing very well. Our solicitor, such a nice man, came to see me. He's dealing with everything. And the money's all right because I have a bank account of my own — my family set up a trust of some sort for me years ago. Desmond always saw to that and just gave me the housekeeping money every month. But now, of course, I can take money out and buy things myself."

"I see. That's all right, then." I was feeling slightly embarrassed by all this personal information and wanted to change the subject. "Oh, by the way, I have a cat basket you can borrow if you'd like."

"That's so kind of you, Sheila, but I think I'd better buy one — I'll need to take him to the vet for other things, won't I? But if you've got a book about looking after cats, I'd really like to borrow that. I couldn't find anything useful in the library."

"Yes, of course. I've got several. I'll bring them round for you."

"It would be lovely to see you, but if you don't have time to make the journey, you could give them to me at the shop."

"You're going back there?" I asked.

"Oh yes. I enjoy working there; I wouldn't want to give it up."

"But do you think you'll be all right — I mean, after what's happened? Are you sure you can face it?"

"Life goes on — isn't that what they say?"

"Well, yes. But these are — well, exceptional circumstances."

"You think people might be shocked?" she asked.

"Not shocked exactly, but embarrassed perhaps."

"I hadn't thought of that — I wouldn't want to upset anyone. Perhaps I'd better leave it for a bit. Perhaps I could collect the books from you — I'd love to see your cottage."

"Yes, do come, anytime." Suddenly I felt I really wanted to get away. I stood up. "I really ought to be getting on. Thank you so much for the coffee. And it was so nice to see Tiger."

"Honestly," I said to Rosemary, "it was really weird! All right, she obviously was completely dominated by horrible Desmond (and, yes, I will speak ill of the dead), but we were all under the impression she adored him. But the extraordinary way she was going on, almost as if he'd just vanished into thin air and wasn't there anymore. No sign of being upset — almost as if she hadn't taken in the fact that he was *killed.* And that flood of conversation. More than I've ever heard her say the whole time I've known her!"

"Grief takes people in funny ways," Rosemary said.

"It wasn't like that. No grieving — well, she was obviously upset that first day when I took her home. Well, no, not upset exactly; more stunned — and worried! But now she's positively cheerful."

"Well, perhaps she hated him and is glad he's dead."

"No, it wasn't that either, not really. She mentioned him a couple of times — things he wouldn't let her do — but there was no emotion of any kind. It was as if she'd completely wiped him out of her life."

"What about John?"

"Still not there. I really can't understand that. They seemed so close. I gather he'll be back for the funeral, whenever that might be, but you'd think he'd want to be there for her."

"Very odd. She didn't say if the police have any idea who might have killed him?"

"No, like I said, she seemed completely uninterested in anything to do with that."

"Lots of people disliked Desmond, but surely not enough to kill him."

"I don't think it was premeditated," I said. "He seems to have been killed with the knife that was lying about in the storeroom. It looks as if someone just snatched it up and stabbed him in the heat of the moment. Of course, it might have been a robbery that went wrong." I told Rosemary about the missing money.

"How much would it have been?" she asked.

"It was midweek and out of season, so probably not more than about four hundred. Desmond was complaining about our sales figures."

"Not a lot to kill someone for."

"I suppose whoever it was panicked. Anyway, I may hear something more when I go in tomorrow. Incidentally, Wendy was all set to come back herself. I persuaded her to give it a bit more time — think how embarrassed everyone would have been!"

"Really most peculiar."

"Oh, well. It will give her more time to be with her cat. That seems to be all she cares about."

But when I went into the shop the following day, no one had heard anything, not even Norma.

"No, the police seem to be making very little progress — as far as I know. Inspector

Morris hasn't seen fit to give me any information, though I would have thought it would only have been polite, considering my position, to have kept me informed." Then, as an afterthought: "How was Wendy; has *she* heard anything?"

"No," I said. "She seems to be all right," I added.

"Poor soul," Norma said. "I can't think how she will manage without Desmond — she was completely dependent on him. It's always very sad when the wife depends on the husband so entirely. How will Wendy cope when she's never been used to doing the simplest thing for herself? I wonder," she said, "if I should go round and see what I can do for her. The funeral, for instance — she's bound to need help with that!"

"That won't be for a while," I said hastily, "and John will be there to help."

Somehow I felt Wendy wouldn't want people (especially Norma) to know that John hadn't come home, and the last thing she (or anyone else, for that matter) would want would be Norma organizing anything.

"Well, I *am* very busy at the moment — so much to do, as you can imagine — but I wouldn't want Wendy to think that I was too busy to help in any way I can. Now, Sheila, perhaps you would be good enough to sort through those piles of T-shirts and put out the inferior ones for disposal."

I went through into the back room — reluctantly, I must admit — but everything looked perfectly normal. It was hard to think it had been the scene of such a violent act. Jean was there, putting clothes on hangers.

"How's her ladyship? I came in here to escape — she's very miffed that the inspector hasn't seen fit to take her into his confidence."

"I know — especially 'in her position.' "

I turned over a pile of T-shirts. "These are all in a muddle — I did sort them last week. I can't find that rather fancy one with the pheasants. I wanted to buy it for Michael."

"Perhaps Madam has removed it as being politically incorrect — blood sports and all that. Oh, I meant to ask — how's poor little Wendy?"

"She seems OK. Quite good, in fact."

"Oh well," Jean said. "Perhaps now Desmond's gone we might get to see the real Wendy at last."

"I wouldn't be surprised," I said.

CHAPTER SEVEN

I was just leaving Brunswick Lodge when Anthea cornered me and thrust a bundle of magazines into my hand.

"Oh, Sheila, would you mind taking these to Miss Paget? I promised them to her last week but I've been so busy."

"Miss Paget?" I asked, feeling, as I always did, resentful that Anthea never imagined that anyone except herself could be busy.

"Yes, you know her. Nice little soul, used to keep the wool shop."

"Oh yes, of course. I didn't realize she was still around. I loved going in there to buy wool — so cozy, it always reminded me of *Alice Through the Looking Glass.*" Anthea looked at me blankly. "You know," I said, "the sheep."

"Oh — well — it's an estate agent's now. But Miss Paget still lives in the flat over the shop. She's more or less housebound, but there's one of those entry phone things so she can let you in."

"But I was just . . ."

"Thanks so much. I must dash!"

Typical Anthea. As it happened there wasn't really anything I needed to do, so I thought I might as well take the magazines around right away. I don't greatly care for entry phones or answer phones or any of the technical devices that seem to have taken over life these days, and when I pressed the entry button there was no reply for a long time. Then an anxious voice said, "Who is it?" and I said, "It's Sheila Malory, Miss Paget. I've brought some magazines for you." Another long wait. Then a click and I was able to open the door and climb the steep stairs and knock on the door at the top. The voice said, "Come in," and there was Miss Paget, sitting in a chair by the window, a small worktable by her side, where she had just laid down a piece of knitting.

"Oh, Mrs. Malory, this is a nice surprise. I haven't seen you since I don't know when. Do sit down and make yourself at home. Forgive me if I don't get up — I find moving about a bit difficult these days."

I moved a chair nearer to hers and said, "How are you keeping?"

"Oh, I'm all right, you know — don't get

about much now."

"I see you're still knitting," I said.

"I like to keep something on the go, just to keep my hand in. Fortunately, it's only my poor old knees that have given way these days. How about you? Did you ever finish that waistcoat with the cable stitch?"

"Goodness!" I exclaimed. "Fancy you remembering that! No, I'm ashamed to say I gave up on it — in spite of all your splendid instructions. I never really got the hang of it."

She smiled. "Such a pity — it was a very popular pattern. Your mother was a very good knitter, I seem to remember."

"Yes, she loved it, until the arthritis got too bad. I always remember a knitted dress she made for me when I was quite small — it was lovely, with openwork panels in the skirt."

"And you don't do much yourself now, then?"

"I'm afraid I never seem to have the time. I would have made something for my granddaughter, but girls don't really like hand-knitted things now." I laid the magazines down on one of the many small tables. "Anthea asked me to bring these along," I said. "She's sorry she wasn't able to come herself."

"She's always in a rush," Miss Paget said. "Always in a hurry, never stays for a cup of tea or anything — such a busy life she leads! Now, you'll stay for a cup, won't you? It's a real treat to see a new face."

"That would be lovely," I said. "Can I do anything to help?" I added as Miss Paget heaved herself with some difficulty out of her chair.

"No, my dear, I'm all right. It's just getting up — there now, I'll go and put the kettle on."

While she was in the kitchen I went and looked out of the window. Miss Paget's sitting room was at the back and looked out over the network of little alleys that connected a lot of the streets in the center of Taviscombe. At this time of day there was quite a lot of activity, people coming and going. To my surprise I saw Norma going through one of the gates and into the yard beyond and I realized that I was looking at the back entrance of the charity shop. Miss Paget called out from the kitchen, and I went in to help her carry the tray of tea things into the sitting room. When she had poured the tea ("I'm sorry it's in a mug, dear, but it's easier when you're on your own") and was sitting down, I took my tea and went over and stood beside her by the

96

window.

"You've got a very good view of what goes on from here," I said.

She laughed. "Oh yes — I call it my window on the world. I can't get out much nowadays but I do like to see all the people going by. I sit here most of the day. Do you know, I can sometimes tell what time it is by what's going on. The children coming and going to school, and some of the deliverymen always deliver at the same time — a couple of them always look up and wave to me!"

"It must be very interesting."

"It is — people used to say to me, Wouldn't you like a nice cottage in the country? But I always said to them, no, I like watching people, not cows and sheep! No, as long as I can look out of my window in the day and watch my programs in the evening, I'm perfectly happy."

"I hadn't realized that you can see the back of the charity shop from here," I said. "I've been working there for a while."

"Yes, I often see people going in and out from there. But what a dreadful thing *that* was, that poor man. I read all about it in the *Gazette.* It must have been very upsetting for you all."

"It has been most upsetting." I finished

my tea and put the mug down. "I don't suppose you happened to notice anything special that day?"

"What day would that be?"

"It was a Thursday, the fourteenth. I don't suppose you remember?"

"Oh yes. The fourteenth was my dear father's birthday, so I always have some little treat — it was some very nice raspberries a kind friend brought me. She knows I like to have a little celebration, as you might say — and some cream to go with them. Wasn't that kind!"

"How lovely. But were you watching in the afternoon — after four thirty, say."

"After four thirty," she said slowly. "It's usually quite quiet then — the children have gone home after school and people don't seem to shop much in the late afternoon, do they — or if they do they go to the supermarket outside the town."

"So did you see anyone going in and out?"

She drank a little of her tea. "Well now, let me see. There was a young man round about then. I remember him specially. He hung about outside for a while before he went in — I thought that was a bit odd — and he wasn't in there very long and then he came out in a great hurry and rushed away. I wondered at the time what *that* was

98

all about — you do think about the unusual things you've seen, don't you, especially when you're on your own all the time."

"And was he the only person who went in?" I asked.

"Oh no, dear. A while after that there was a gentleman, very smart in a business suit. He didn't seem sure of the right door — he was counting the doors in the alley to make sure he'd got the right one. I'd never seen *him* before, although, now I come to think of it, I do remember seeing the young man once or twice."

"Did he stay long?"

"Longer than the young man, but not what you'd call a long time."

"And that was all?"

"The last person I saw was the lady — but she used to be there often."

"You mean one of the ladies who worked there?"

"I don't think so — I only ever saw her in the late afternoon."

"What did she look like?"

"Oh dear, let me think. Tall, dark haired, neatly dressed."

"About how old?"

"Not young, more or less middle-aged."

"And how long did she stay?"

"She was usually there quite a while. But

I don't often see her go because it's time for my program — I don't like to miss that."

I went back and sat down beside her. "Miss Paget," I said. "I do think you ought to tell the police everything you saw that day."

"The police — oh no, dear, I don't think I could do that. I wouldn't want to get anyone into trouble."

"No, I'm sure you wouldn't be doing that. But it would be such a help for Inspector Morris to know who was there."

"Inspector Morris? Bob Morris? Grace Morris's son? I remember her very well. She was always in the shop. A lovely knitter — you remember I used to sell made-up garments sometimes? Well, she used to do some of them for me — between ourselves, I think they needed the money. Such a nice woman, so sad she died quite young. Well, fancy young Bob being an inspector — I knew he'd gone into the police force. Hasn't he done well!"

"Yes, hasn't he? So, do you think you could have a chat with him, tell him what you've told me? I'm sure he'd be very grateful."

She was silent for a moment. Then she said, "You really think it would be a help?"

"Oh yes. It's something Bob really needs

to know. It would be a great help."

"Well, I'll do it then. But how do I get in touch? I couldn't phone the police station!"

"It's all right. I'll tell Bob you want to speak to him."

"But you'll be here, too?" she asked anxiously.

"Well, yes, of course, if that's all right with Bob."

"I wouldn't want to do anything *official,* if you know what I mean."

"I'm sure your name would never come into it," I said reassuringly.

She finished her tea. "Fancy Grace's son being an inspector — she'd have been so proud of him. I remember him coming into the shop with her sometimes when he was quite a little boy. It only seems like yesterday — where does the time go to?"

I called in at the police station on my way home and was lucky enough to find Bob Morris there.

"I thought you really ought to know what Miss Paget saw," I said.

"It all happened quite a few days ago; are you sure she remembers exactly what she did see? After all, she is old. She must be well over eighty. Nice old soul — she was very good to my mother. I remember her when I was quite a boy."

"She remembers you, too," I said. "And your mother. As for her memory — well, she even remembered a knitting pattern I gave up on at least ten years ago!" He laughed, and I went on: "No, she sits at that window every day and I'm sure she could tell you what she saw there six months ago. Actually, as it happens, the fourteenth was her father's birthday so she remembered it particularly."

"Well, in that case, it sounds promising. Don't tell me what she said to you. I'd like to get it fresh from her, if you see what I mean."

"Of course. There is one thing, though. She was a bit apprehensive about it — I think that somehow she didn't want people to think that she was spying on them, and she only agreed because she knew you and was fond of your mother. And she did say that she wanted me to be there when she spoke to you. Would that be all right?" He looked a bit doubtful, so I said, "I could be in the kitchen making the tea, if you like. Just as long as she knows I'm there. I'm sure once she gets used to the idea and you've had a bit of a chat about the old days, she'll be fine."

We arranged a time for the following day.

I rang Miss Paget and told her I'd certainly be there, too. Actually, once we were there and she saw Bob Morris ("I'd have known you anywhere — you've got a real look of poor Grace"), she was quite happy so I was able to retreat into the kitchen and leave them to it.

After a while he put his head round the door, gave me a nod and a smile and said, "We're ready for that tea now, Mrs. Malory." I took the tray in and was pleased to see that Miss Paget was quite relaxed and happy to treat it as a social occasion. I thought again how good Bob was with people and was amused to see how well he took Miss Paget's inclination to treat him as the small boy she'd once known.

When we had left the flat he said, "Thank you, Mrs. Malory. That was a real help. Not just who she saw going in and out that particular day, but the general setup, you might say."

"There certainly seems to have been quite a bit going on, presumably every day. I can quite see why Miss Paget was interested — it was like one of her television soap operas!"

He laughed. "She certainly followed it all with interest. I see what you mean about her memory."

"I meant to ask you," I said. "Did you find

that knife at the shop?"

He shook his head. "No sign of it, and no one seems to have seen it."

"So you think that was the weapon?"

"It's a strong possibility."

"You don't think you'll find it?"

"It could be at the bottom of the Bristol Channel," he said. "On the other hand, people don't always behave rationally — the murderer may have kept it. You never know."

"I can see how she'd like it," Rosemary said when I told her all about Miss Paget. "All that coming and going. I just hope that when I'm old, if I'm ever stuck in a chair all day I'd be able to see things going on outside. I always remember going to see my cousin Doris when she was in a home. It was a gorgeous place, right out the other side of Dulverton, wonderful country views, and I was saying to her how beautiful and peaceful it all was and she burst out, 'I don't want peaceful. It's so boring — sometimes I just wish that cow out there would *explode*!' "

I laughed. "I know what she meant. Anyway, Miss Paget at her observation post may have done Wendy a favor."

"Wendy?"

"Yes. I suspect the young man she saw was

Wendy's son, John. And if other people went into the shop after he'd gone, then he couldn't have killed his father."

"You think that was a possibility? Surely not."

"I'm sure Wendy thought so. She was so very keen to say that he'd already gone back to his university at Nottingham that day. But I heard Desmond say he wanted to talk to John when he got home that evening, so *he* assumed John wouldn't have gone back by then."

"You spoke to him on the phone when you took Wendy home the next morning. Would he have had time to get to Nottingham by then? It's a very roundabout journey to get there from Taviscombe — bus to Taunton first and then a couple of changes. . . ."

"I spoke to him on his mobile — he could have been anywhere!"

"That's true."

"I've just thought of something. You know I told you Wendy was so upset — well, numb, really — when I took her back that morning after she'd seen the police? Then the next day when I called she was bright and cheerful. I put that down to all the business about Tiger. But it occurs to me she wasn't upset about Desmond's death but instead was worried because she thought

John might have done it. I think she knew he was going to see his father and she was afraid. . . ."

"That he might have snatched up a knife and killed him?"

"Yes. And *that's* why she was so insistent that he'd already gone back to Nottingham."

"I suppose so. Mind you, from what I've seen of John Barlow, he doesn't look the sort of person to *kill* anyone. Far too feeble," Rosemary observed.

"Desperation perhaps?"

"Perhaps. But I think you're right about Wendy."

"And come to think of it, I saw she'd put a photo of her and John on the mantelpiece when I went the next day. She wouldn't have done that, would she, if she still thought he'd killed his father? I mean, she wouldn't have wanted to draw attention to him in any way."

"True."

"I think she must have got in touch with him after I left and he told her where he was and what he'd been doing, and when she knew he *hadn't* killed his father she was all right."

"You mean she wasn't upset about Desmond's death at all?"

"Well, it was a shock, of course, but I don't think she grieved for him. No, John is the only person she cares about."

"And Tiger."

"And Tiger, of course."

"I suppose," Rosemary said thoughtfully, "just because she was so meek and docile with Desmond we assumed she adored him."

"When, in fact, she was frightened of him and probably hated him in the end."

"You don't suppose she murdered Desmond?"

"No — well, I don't know. Just because I gave her that lift home doesn't necessarily mean that she *stayed* at home. She could have gone back to the shop again if something happened —" I broke off. "I've just remembered something. That first time, when I brought her home — when she went out to make the tea I thought I heard voices and then a door slamming."

"John?"

"It must have been. She didn't mention anyone being there — well, she wouldn't if it was John — *so* he may have told her something that —"

"That made her go back to the shop and murder Desmond?"

"No, something that made her think that

that's what John was going to do and that's why she was so upset!"

CHAPTER EIGHT

I'd just taken the washing out of the machine and was wondering if the sun was going to last long enough to make it worthwhile putting it out on the line when the doorbell rang. It was Wendy.

"Sorry to drop in on you like this," she said, "but you did very kindly say you'd lend me those cat books."

"Of course. Do come in."

"What a lovely cottage — really Old World!" she said as we went into the sitting room.

"It's sixteenth century mostly, though bits kept being burnt down because of the thatch, so parts were added later."

"Sixteenth century — my goodness!"

"Do sit down. Would you like a coffee, or tea if you'd rather?"

"A cup of tea would be lovely." Tris, who always feels it is his duty to greet any visitor, came in and sat at her feet, looking up at her expectantly. "Oh, I didn't know you had a dog as well as a cat," she said. "Isn't he sweet?"

She bent down and made a fuss of him until Tris, having done what he felt was required, went back into the kitchen, where he had been occupied with the remains of a very old bone. Foss, who likes to make an entrance in his own time, advanced towards Wendy, allowed her to stroke him briefly, then turned and leapt onto the windowsill, where he sat bolt upright, his back to the room, apparently absorbed in watching a magpie, an old enemy, though I knew, from the occasional twitching of his tail, he was critically aware of what was going on inside the room.

I found the books and left her to look at them while I got the tea. Somehow I had the feeling — something in her manner — that the books weren't the real reason she'd come. As I poured the tea and cut slices of coffee sponge, we exchanged remarks about Foss ("So beautiful — I don't really know much about Siamese; they say they're more like dogs than cats, don't they?") and Tiger ("He's settled in so well, you'd think he'd lived with me always."), but I found myself waiting for what she really wanted to say.

"How's John?" I asked. "Is he home yet?"

She put down her cup and leaned forward. "I'm so worried, Sheila. He's coming back today — the police rang and said they wanted to talk to him."

"Well," I said. "I suppose it's only natural. . . ."

"He had nothing to do with it — he wasn't here," she said quickly.

"Actually, Wendy," I said, "the police have a witness who saw him going into the back entrance of the shop after we'd all gone."

"Oh no!" she exclaimed. "It can't be — they must have been mistaken."

"No. The police are quite certain."

"But he had nothing to do with — he just wanted to talk to him!" She was becoming so agitated I felt I had to say something to calm her.

"It's all right, Wendy. Look, I shouldn't be telling you this, but they do know Desmond was alive when John left."

"Oh, thank God!" She burst into tears. "Oh, I'm so sorry — it's such a relief. I've been so worried. I *knew* he couldn't have done such a thing. I didn't even have to ask him. But people don't understand. . . ."

"Tell me about it if it would help," I said. "I'll just go and fill up the teapot and we'll have another cup."

I spent a little while in the kitchen to give

her time to recover herself. Foss, discomposed by Wendy's human emotion, had followed me into the kitchen and seized the opportunity to demand and get a handful of cat treats.

"There we are," I said brightly as I went back into the sitting room. "Now then, what happened?"

"They never got on," Wendy said, "even when John was a little boy — he was shy, you see. He took after me. Nothing he did was ever right for Desmond. He did quite well at school, nothing special — well, we moved round the country a bit because of Desmond's job, so poor John never had time to settle properly in one school or make friends. He wasn't any good at games either. He hated them. Desmond never understood that either. I suppose what he wanted was a son like himself. That was *never* going to happen, but he wouldn't believe it. He thought that if he kept on at John he could change him."

"Poor boy."

"John did try," Wendy said earnestly. "He really wanted to please his father. But no matter how much he tried it was never good enough. For some reason Desmond set his mind on wanting John to go in for the law, so there was all this extra coaching to pass exams. The poor boy never had a moment to himself; it was work, work, work all the time, even in the holidays."

"Oh dear."

"John managed to get into university and you'd have thought Desmond would be satisfied, but no, the pressure still carried on. Honestly, Sheila, I thought he was heading for a breakdown."

"It must have been awful for you. I suppose you couldn't persuade Desmond to ease up a bit?"

She gave a little laugh. "I might as well have spoken to a brick wall. He never listened to what I said, even for the little things. No, the thing that kept John sane was his drawing. Though I say it myself, he's got a real gift that way. He never let his father know, of course — Desmond would soon have put a stop to that."

"Surely he'd have been proud of something his son did well."

"Not if it wasn't *his* sort of thing. I remember when John was a little boy at school he brought home a picture he'd done. It was the best in the class, and he was so pleased so he brought it home to show us. All Desmond said was he wasn't paying school fees to have his son waste time on that sort of rubbish."

"Poor child."

"Anyway, things came to a head when John had to go back to university this term. There'd be exams and he knew he wasn't going to do well in them. He was really frightened of his father — we both were — and he felt he couldn't go on. Anyway, when he was at school in Birmingham (we were there for a time for Desmond's job), the art master, such a nice man, thought really highly of John's work. So without telling anyone, even me, John got in touch with this master and, to cut a long story short, he managed to get John into the art school there."

"Goodness."

"Well, you can imagine how I felt. I really wanted John to take it up, but I knew what a dreadful row there'd be. That day, you may have heard him, Desmond said he wanted to speak to John when he got home — something about extra work before the exams, I think it was — and that was too much for John. He said he was going to have it out with his father once and for all and that he'd go to Birmingham and leave home for good."

"John was there, wasn't he, when I gave you a lift home that day? I heard voices when you went out to make the tea."

"I was trying to persuade him just to go, without seeing his father, but he was quite determined. He had a bag and his portfolio already packed. He left them in the yard when he went in to see his father." She paused. "He said it was terrible — things were said. . . . Desmond said he could never come back home and he'd make sure John never saw me again, things like that. John couldn't stand any more — he just left, got the bus to Taunton and the train to Birmingham. He's staying in a hotel there for a bit. He phoned that night to tell me what happened."

"So that's where he was when I spoke to him on the phone — when I told him about his father?"

"Yes, he was dreadfully upset — for me, really. He wanted to come home, but I wouldn't let him — well, if anyone knew about that row with his father, they might think. . . ."

"But it will be all right now. As long as he tells the police exactly what happened. Like I said, they know Desmond was alive when John left."

Wendy got to her feet. "I must go," she said. "I must go and meet his train at Taunton — I can drive there. I must catch him before he goes to the police — he might do that before coming home. Now I can tell him it's going to be all right."

"As long as he tells the police the truth."

"Yes, yes, I'll tell him." She was moving towards the door.

"Don't forget the cat books," I said.

"Well!" Rosemary said when I brought her up to date about Wendy's visit. "It must have taken John quite a nerve to confront his father like that. Though I suppose there comes a point when you just can't stand things any longer. Even someone as wimpish as John."

"Still," I said, "everything's going to be all right for him now. He can go to art college. I wonder if Wendy will move to Birmingham to be near him. I think she'd quite like to get rid of that house."

"What I still can't understand," Rosemary said thoughtfully, "is even when she'd heard from John about what had happened and where he was, she still doesn't seem to have been worried when Desmond didn't come home that night."

"She might have gone to bed early so as not to have to face him when he got in — after all that had happened, I mean — and just fallen asleep."

"I suppose. . . ."

"And the police appear to have phoned her very early the next morning."

"You may be right, but it still seems pretty odd to me."

"Everything about that marriage seems pretty odd," I said.

We were a bit short staffed at the shop since Wendy, obviously, hadn't come back yet, and Norma was in a particularly bossy mood, ordering Jean and me about "as if we're her paid servants," as Jean said bitterly. She joined me in the storeroom when Norma was occupied with a customer.

"I can't stand much more of this," she said. "She's just told me I've marked up that latest batch of things from Mrs. Turner — I beg your pardon, the *Honorable* Mrs. Turner — wrong because they're mostly designer labels. Well, of course I know that; I'm not a fool. I used the list to check them, like we always do. But oh no, that wasn't enough for Madam! She gave me one of her Little Talks, you know, all patronizing. Have you noticed how when she wants to make you feel really stupid, she makes you sit down so that she can *tower* over you to make you feel small!" She moved over to the kitchen. "Well, I'm going to make a cup of tea, and if she doesn't like it she can lump it."

She put the kettle on and got out the mugs.

"By the way, Sheila, did the inspector ask you about that knife I was using — you know, the one I had to open that box of cards?"

"Yes, he did, as a matter of fact."

"He asked me a lot about that — I don't know if he asked Norma; she didn't deign to tell me if he did — and he turned the place upside down looking for it. I suppose he thinks that was used to kill Desmond."

"It certainly looks like it."

She shivered. "It gives me a sort of creepy feeling. You know — the next person to pick it up was a murderer!"

"Try not to think about it," I said soothingly.

"And another thing, when they find it my fingerprints will be on it!"

"Well, they're not going to think you killed him."

"There were times when I felt like it," Jean said vehemently. "And right now I'd like to do the same to Madam!" She caught herself up. "No, I shouldn't say things like that — not after what's happened." She put the tea bags into the mugs and poured the water onto them. "Help yourself to milk. Sheila, you know this inspector what's-his-name . . . Morris. What does he think about it?"

"I don't know, I'm afraid. It's early days yet, and I suppose they have to eliminate everyone who might have had a reason to kill him."

"Like poor little Wendy, or that son of theirs. Not that they'd have the nerve to do it."

"There may be all sorts of people — we don't really know much about him or who he might have upset."

"That's true. Actually, there was a gentleman in one day last week asking for him. A stranger — well, I'd never seen him before."

"Really? What was he like?"

"Well spoken, some sort of businessman, he was wearing a suit. At first I thought he might be here to value those pictures, but he wasn't the usual person."

"What did he say?"

"He just asked if Desmond was here. I said he wasn't at the moment but he'd probably be in late afternoon."

"Did he ask for Desmond or Mr. Barlow?"

"I can't remember — yes, I can. He asked for Mr. Barlow, so I thought at the time he probably wasn't a friend and that's why I wondered about the pictures."

"Did you tell the inspector about him?"

"No, should I have done? I hadn't thought about him until this moment."

"I think he ought to know, especially if you think he was a stranger."

Jean put two spoonfuls of sugar in her mug and stirred it vigorously. "Well, I'll tell him if he comes in again — I expect he will. I can't be bothered to go traipsing all the way up to the police station."

Norma came into the storeroom, pointedly ignored our mugs of tea, and said, "Perhaps one of you could spare the time to come and take over in the shop. I have to go to the printer to see if that new poster I ordered is ready — they should have delivered it yesterday and I need it for the new window display."

I put down my mug and followed her into the shop.

"I believe you are in touch with Wendy," she said. "Has she said anything about when she might be coming back?"

"She hasn't said, but I wouldn't think until after the funeral. It will be very distressing for her."

"Naturally, and normally I wouldn't inquire, but we have been very busy lately — morbid curiosity in some cases, which, of course, I deplore, but that doesn't alter the fact that we need a full staff to cope with things."

"Well, she has her son back home now and they will have all sorts of things to arrange. . . ."

"I quite understand that, but I would be grateful if, when you are in touch with her next, you would inquire — tactfully, of course — if she does intend coming back. If not, then I do feel we must replace her as soon as possible. As a matter of fact, I have a very suitable person in mind. She has only just come to Taviscombe but she has had a great deal of experience in the retail trade."

"Really."

"She ran a very successful antiques shop in Malvern, so she would be invaluable to us for valuing the china and porcelain."

"Why did she leave Malvern for Taviscombe?" I inquired idly.

Norma gave me a cold look. "Her husband has relatives down here, I believe. He plays golf with Marcus, and we have been to dinner with them several times."

"Well, I'll see if I can find out what Wendy wants to do. . . ."

"Excellent. One more thing. I imagine Inspector Morris has spoken to you about that knife. He consulted me about it, of course, and I told him how distressed I was

121

that Jean had left it lying about like that. Quite inexcusable. Even if this dreadful thing hadn't happened. I can't think what the health and safety people will say. I haven't said anything to Jean myself — no doubt the police will have told her how reprehensible it was and how, in a way, she is responsible for this whole sorry affair."

"Oh, I don't really think —"

"Right, well, I'll be off. I'll leave you in charge. I won't be long." She put on her coat, picked up her handbag and swept out. As the shop door closed, Jean put her head round the door.

"Has she gone? Here's your tea — it had got a bit cold but I hotted it up in the microwave."

"Oh, thanks. She's gone to the printer to get that poster she designed for the window."

"She couldn't wait to change the window display, could she? Desmond barely cold in his grave — not that he is in his grave yet. Have you heard anything about the funeral?"

"No. They'll have to wait until the police can release the body."

"I suppose Wendy will have to see to all the arrangements. I wonder how she'll cope with that?"

"At least she'll have John to help her," I said.

"I wouldn't think *he'd* be much use, from what I've seen of him."

"I think she has a nice solicitor. I expect he can see to things."

"I suppose we'll be expected to go — to the funeral, I mean."

"I think Wendy would appreciate it."

"It'll be at that church of his — there'll be all that crowd." She finished her tea and put down her mug. "It's just occurred to me. Norma's such a one for doing things by the book — do you think she's put Desmond's death in the accident book!"

CHAPTER NINE

Wendy's "nice solicitor" turned out to be Nigel Forest, one of Michael's friends in another practice.

"You know Wendy Barlow, don't you?" Michael asked when he came to bring me some more eggs. "Doesn't she work at that charity shop of yours?"

"Yes, I know Wendy. Why?"

"Poor Nigel's having a difficult time with her."

"I'd never have called Wendy difficult," I said. "She's far too poor-spirited!"

"Not difficult like that, but Nigel's trying to settle her husband's estate, and whenever he asks her even the simplest question she just says, 'Oh, Desmond did all that.'"

"Well, he did. Dealt with everything. He just doled out the housekeeping money every week or whenever, and that's all she ever knew about it. Apparently there's a sort of trust."

"Indeed there is," Michael said. "I gather she's a very wealthy woman."

"Good heavens!"

"Nigel couldn't believe that anyone in this day and age could know so little about their financial situation."

"If he'd ever seen them together he'd have understood. But he must have known Desmond and seen what a control freak he was."

"Well, yes, but even so . . ."

"He'd got her to the state where she didn't have a mind of her own."

"She's got no idea of anything — Nigel's having to arrange the funeral and everything."

"Presumably Desmond left a will?"

"Oh yes — he couldn't do anything about the trust, of course, but he left a couple of quite substantial legacies to people outside the family."

"Who . . . I don't suppose you can tell me?"

"No. But I can tell you that Nigel was surprised that he left nothing to his son."

"He really was a loathsome man!" I said.

Michael gathered up the empty egg boxes I'd put aside for him. "Oh, by the way, Thea says some of the eggs are from the new bantams. They're quite small, but the yolks are proper size; it's just the whites that are smaller."

"So they've fixed the funeral then," Rosemary said. "I suppose all you lot from the shop will be going?"

"We thought we'd like to support poor Wendy."

"I'd like to tag along, if you don't mind. I wanted to have a word with her, but I didn't like to call or ring."

"Well, there's the usual 'do' afterwards in the church hall, so you can have a word then."

St. Mary's church was almost full. Most of the parishioners had come to pay their last respects; some, perhaps, with a slightly guilty feeling of relief. Most of our group from the shop (and Rosemary) sat modestly at the back of the church, but I noticed, with some amusement, that Norma and Marcus firmly seated themselves in one of the front pews, though Marcus looked rather embarrassed. After a while they were joined by a middle-aged woman dressed in black who sat a little apart from them.

"Who's that?" Rosemary whispered. "A relative of some sort?"

Jean, who was sitting next to us, shook her head. "No, that's Desmond's lady friend from St. Mary's."

Rosemary was obviously longing to inquire further, but just then the coffin was carried in, followed by Wendy and John, who stood uncertainly in the aisle until they were shepherded into their front pew by Nigel, who seemed to be in attendance. It was a good service, and thanks to the large congregation, the hymns were given full value in energy and volume, which is not always the case. The vicar paid a handsome tribute to "a man who has contributed so much to this parish," and everyone felt, I'm sure, that things had been done properly.

After the committal we all trooped into the church hall, which was pleasantly overheated after the chill outside. There were plates of food spread out on the trestle tables, and the urn and the cups and saucers were laid out in rows. In fact, it looked just like it did on our last visit for the produce sale. There was the same hum of conversation, not noticeably different in volume and animation. Indeed there was a positive absence of the usual hushed tones and mumbled expressions of sorrow.

Jean attached herself to Rosemary and me (Margaret and Dorothy were talking to Wendy, and Norma had buttonholed the vicar) as we all went to get our sandwiches and coffee. After we were settled at a table,

Rosemary turned to Jean and said, "What *did* you mean about Desmond's lady friend?"

Jean shrugged. "Oh, it's no secret. Edna says everyone knew about Agnes Davis and Desmond."

"You mean they're having an affair?" I asked.

"No one's ever worked that one out. I mean, it wouldn't be easy. He's married and she lives with her elderly mother. Anyway, can you imagine a cold fish like Desmond going in for anything as passionate as an affair! No, I think it was all on a high intellectual plane, long discussions about the Prayer Book Service and Series Three."

"Did Wendy know about it?" Rosemary asked.

"Oh yes."

"And she didn't mind?"

"She certainly wouldn't have the courage to say anything if she did," I said.

"She was probably grateful to Agnes," Jean said, "for keeping him occupied and out of the house in the evening."

"The evening?"

"Agnes sometimes used to come round to the shop after we were shut. I found out about that when I forgot my umbrella and had to go back for it. His Lordship was *very* put out and muttered something about her bringing him some parish magazines, but she obviously couldn't have cared less — gave me a very haughty stare, daring me to think anything!"

"She's talking to the vicar now," I said, looking at the black-clad figure. "It's funny really — she's in deepest mourning and Wendy is just wearing her usual tweed coat."

"I expect she sees herself as Desmond's real widow. Come to think of it, she'll probably miss him more than Wendy will."

Just then Edna Palmer came up to speak to us.

"You managed to get here, then — quite a good turnout. Pretty well everyone — except those he'd offended, of course. I thought Reverend Nicholas spoke very well, considering. I mean, you can't tell me he isn't glad to have his parish to himself again. And poor little Wendy — I bet she feels she's been let out of prison!"

"Agnes will miss him," Jean said.

Edna gave a short laugh. "Oh, she'll miss him all right. Just look at her done up like that — I'm surprised she hasn't got a veil, the lot! I see she's making up to the reverend now. She didn't have a good word to say for him when her precious Desmond was alive. How he didn't appreciate all the hard work

129

that dear Desmond was doing, how he was always off on these exchanges and so forth. As if he ever got a look in with that man always pushing himself forward."

"Poor Mr. Nicholas," Rosemary said, "if she's got her sights on him."

"Oh, the reverend's no fool. He's very good at offloading overenthusiastic parishioners, very diplomatically, of course. No, I expect she'll go to All Saints; they've got a young vicar there who won't know how to shake her off!"

Rosemary got up. "I just want to have a quick word with Wendy. Then we must be off."

I joined her and left Jean and Edna to enjoy their chat.

Wendy, who had been saying good-bye to some of the parishioners, was standing by herself near the door. She seemed to be deep in thought, and for a moment we hesitated to disturb her, but then Rosemary went forward and said the usual things about loss and sympathy and so on. Wendy seemed to collect herself and greeted us both warmly.

"It's so good to see a friendly face," she said. "No, I don't mean that exactly — everyone's been very kind, but they" — she gestured towards the people in the hall —

"are only here because of the church, if you see what I mean, because it's the right thing to do."

"It was nice to see the church full," I ventured. "I'm sure Desmond would have been very pleased."

"Oh *he* would."

"Where is John?" Rosemary asked. "You must be so glad to have him here at this time."

"Oh, he had a headache so I sent him home," Wendy said. "He can see to Tiger — I don't like leaving him alone for too long."

"Is John going back to Birmingham?" I asked. "And will you go with him?"

"It's all right for John to go, but Mr. Forest said I ought not to go, too, until the police have found out more about who killed Desmond. So it will be just Tiger and me."

"It's nice for you to have company," Rosemary said, but Wendy seemed impervious to any hint of irony.

"Yes, well, animals are better than humans sometimes, aren't they?" she said.

Rosemary suddenly nudged me and indicated a man farther down the hall. It was the man we'd seen at the produce show.

"Wendy," Rosemary said, "who is that man, over there talking to the vicar? His face seems familiar."

"Oh, that's George Arnold," Wendy said. "He used to work with Desmond. Fancy him being here."

As we spoke he caught Wendy's eye and came over.

"My dear Wendy," he said. "I was so distressed to hear the sad news. You must be devastated. I can hardly believe it — I saw him quite recently in this very place. We had such a splendid chat. . . ."

His voice went on, smooth as his manner, and I felt we should really be moving tactfully away. But Rosemary stood firm, nodding her head sympathetically from time to time, indeed showing more response than Wendy.

"Well," he said, taking Wendy's hand and holding it in both of his. "Do please let me know if there's anything I can do for you — any of Desmond's business papers that need sorting — anything at all I can do to help. You have my number. Do ring, and I'll be in touch soon to see how things are going." He let go of her hand, which she allowed to fall limply at her side, and he gave a slight nod to us. "So nice to have met you. . . ." And he went away.

"Did he work with Desmond for a long time?" Rosemary asked.

"George? Oh yes, they go back a long way. I wonder how he knew about Desmond."

"Perhaps Nigel — Mr. Forest — put a notice in the *Times* or the *Telegraph,*" I suggested.

"That will be it," she said. "He's been so kind."

"Well," Rosemary said. "We must be off."

"How will you get home?" I asked.

"Norma said —" Wendy broke off as Norma came up to us.

"Well, then, Wendy, I think you might leave now. Most people have gone or will be going. It should be all right if you just have a word with Mr. Nicholas — just a word to thank him. Then we can drive you home."

Wendy, who had been quite animated when speaking to us, became the subdued, docile creature she was when with Desmond. "Yes, of course," she said meekly. "If you think that will be all right."

"Well, I think everything went off very well," Norma said as Wendy went over obediently to speak to the vicar. "Quite a good congregation, and the vicar spoke most suitably. Marcus and I will just see her back home and make sure everything is as it should be."

"John is at home now," I said.

Norma smiled condescendingly. "I'm sure

he is very devoted to his mother, but I hardly think he is a great deal of practical help. Now, then," she went on as Wendy came back. "Have you got your hat? You didn't wear one? Oh well, never mind; we'll be off. You will be in tomorrow as usual, Sheila? That's right. Come along, then. Marcus is just fetching the car — so difficult parking here."

She walked briskly away, Wendy trailing behind her.

"Oh dear," Rosemary said. "Poor Wendy, exchanging one tyrant for another! 'Everything went off very well'! Just as though *she* arranged it all."

"Typical Norma," I said. "Still, I somehow don't think Wendy will come back to the shop, and Norma has too many other irons in the fire to bother with Wendy if she's not under her eye. Anyway, let's get out of here. Come back with me and we'll have a proper cup of tea."

I fed the animals, let them out into the garden and made the tea.

"I wonder what that man Arnold wanted," Rosemary said, "that time we saw him before."

"I think he must have been the man Miss Paget saw going in to see Desmond after

John had left."

"But if this Agnes person went in after *he* left, then he couldn't have killed Desmond — well, not unless she found the body and stayed there to keep a vigil over it!"

"Yes. Very funny. No, but even if he didn't kill Desmond, he may know about something they were both mixed up in that might have been the reason for his death."

"Well, I get the feeling he's frightened about something," Rosemary said. "Well, nervous, anyway. All that smarming over Wendy and offering to look over Desmond's business papers. That wasn't just a helpful gesture. No, he thinks there may be something there. . . ."

"What sort of something?"

"I don't know — something illegal, perhaps, that they were both mixed up in."

"I don't see Desmond being mixed up in anything illegal somehow."

"Well, dodgy somehow. Are you going to tell Bob Morris about him?"

"I think so. And I can tell him about Agnes at the same time."

"I suppose she *was* the mysterious female?"

"Oh, I'd think so. Wouldn't you? Unless Desmond had two lady friends."

"It's a great pity Miss Paget went to watch

her program and didn't see her leave. Then we'd know."

"Know what?" I asked. "Oh, surely you don't think Agnes killed him!"

"Well, you never can tell with odd people like that. She may have been jealous. . . ."

"No, really! But I suppose we can't be positive it was her. 'Tall, middle-aged' — it could have been anyone."

"Someone from the shop? Miss Paget said it was someone she'd seen before."

"Well, Norma's tall, and so is Margaret, but I can't imagine what reason either of them would have to kill him. I know Norma never got on with him, but still. . . . Anyway, she went home early with a headache — at least that's what she said, though I think she really went off in a huff."

"How bad a huff?"

"*Not* bad enough to murder him!"

"Wendy's quite tall."

"Oh, come on! Poor little soul!"

"Driven to desperation?"

"Possibly. But she was at home — I drove her there myself."

"She could have got a bus back after you'd left. The time would fit in."

"Well, yes," I admitted reluctantly. "It is possible. Oh, I don't know — I'm all confused now. I'll simply tell Bob Morris about

136

Agnes and the Arnold man and he can speak to them and find out if they were there."

I telephoned the police station and left a message. Bob came round the next afternoon. We seemed to gravitate naturally to the kitchen, and I automatically put the kettle on and got out the cake tin. He listened carefully to what I had to tell him about Agnes and George Arnold and asked a few questions.

Then he said, "Inspector Eliot always used to say how much he relied on you to fill him in on details. About people especially — he said you noticed things."

I laughed. "I expect he also mentioned my insatiable curiosity," I said.

"He didn't put it quite like that, but he did say how helpful it was."

"Well, I suppose people are always extra careful what they say to the police, even when they're off duty — a sort of invisible barrier. They're more relaxed with someone they chat to more or less every day. And, of course, I've lived here all my life so I know a great many people — I've watched a lot of them grow up."

"That helps."

"Well, it means you're more aware of the relationships between them, if you know what I mean. Mind you, I really don't know that much about Desmond Barlow. We only had a sort of nodding acquaintance before I went to work at the shop."

"I think you had him pretty well summed up."

"If you mean did I feel that he was an unpleasant control freak — well, I think that was the impression of everyone who came into contact with him!"

"That does seem to be the general opinion. But seriously, Mrs. Malory, it would be a help if we could have a chat from time to time, just to compare notes, you might say."

"Of course. My son says I'm always delighted to give my opinion on anything, even without being asked."

Bob laughed. "And talking of sons, I was wondering if you'd mind calling in on Dad sometime. I've mentioned that I've seen you recently, and he was inquiring after you. I know he'd really appreciate a chat if you could spare the time."

"Of course, I'd love to. When would be a good time?"

"Well any day, really. He doesn't get out much, only to the doctor and so on nowadays. Mornings are best; he usually has a rest in the afternoon."

"How about Tuesday morning — about

eleven, if that's all right?"

"That's fine. He'll be looking forward to it."

"And so will I. Now, the kettle's boiled. How about that cup of tea?"

CHAPTER TEN

I was shocked to see how much worse poor Reg Morris had become. He now moved slowly and leaned heavily on a walking frame. He led the way along the hall, through the dining room and into a small conservatory.

"I usually sit in here in the mornings," he said, "to catch the sun."

"It's beautifully warm," I replied. "And how lovely all your flowers are!"

"Well, I can't do anything out-of-doors, but I potter about in here — it keeps me going."

"Those glorious begonias — such wonderful colors. Oh, and look at that amazing standard fuchsia! Did you train it yourself?"

"It takes a bit of patience, but it's come on a treat. Come and sit down." He gestured to the two easy chairs that, with a small table, took up a lot of the floor space, the rest being dominated by a large workbench that ran round one side.

I laid some magazines down on the bench and said, "Just a few gardening magazines — I hope you haven't got them already."

"That's kind. I'll like looking at them. Reading and the wireless, that's what I enjoy — not this old television. There's nothing there for the likes of me — all this young stuff."

"Not even the gardening programs?"

"Not what I call gardening," he said scornfully. "A lot of fancy nonsense — you never see them get their hands dirty. No, *Gardeners' Question Time* on the wireless and proper music — those big bands, like we used to have in the war, that's what I like." He sat down in the other chair and indicated the tray on the table. "Betty made some coffee and put it in a flask. If you'd pour it — my hands aren't too steady these days."

I poured the coffee and passed a cup over to him.

"Now, you try one of those flapjacks. Betty made them. She's a proper cook; Bob's been very lucky. And they've got two little ones, a boy, Jimmy, after her dad, and a girl, Gracie, after Bob's mother — you remember her."

"Of course I do — that's really nice."

"She's a good girl, Betty. Looks after me, bless her; calls in every day. I always say without her and Bob I'd be stuck away in one of those homes."

"That's really good to hear. But Reg, I'm sorry to see you so disabled. What is it, arthritis?"

"It's a bit of what old Dr. Dark used to call the screws, but it's mostly my hip. They say it's gone."

"Couldn't you have a hip replacement? They're very good; I know several people who've had them."

"Bob and Betty are always on to me about it, but I say I'm too old for that sort of thing."

"Now, that's nonsense. Lots of people older than you have had them most successfully. Come to think of it, the Queen Mother had hers done when she was nearly a hundred."

"It's all very well for them. Mind you, I've got a lot of time for the royals — though I wouldn't want their job, not for a thousand pounds — but there's all the looking after when you come out. I wouldn't want to be a burden on Betty, and Bob's always busy with his job."

"I'm sure you could go into a care home — the council has several places in Taviscombe — until you were fit to come home. And then," I said, "you'd be able to do so much more for yourself."

He looked unconvinced. "I'm not sure about those places. When I was able to get about I used to go to this day center."

"And what was it like?"

"Them as ran it were all right and the food wasn't bad — they gave you your mid-day meal — but some of the helpers I couldn't be doing with. Wanted you to do exercises and join in singsongs and play bingo. All right for a lot of old women, but not for me!"

"No, I think you are probably better off in your lovely conservatory."

He nodded. "And that's what I told them."

I laughed. "You always were one for speaking your mind."

"I'm all right as I am. Seeing after my plants; and Betty always stays for a chat when she comes and she brings the little ones sometimes. Gracie's still a toddler, but Jimmy's just started school and, mark my words, he's going to be a bright lad, just like his father."

"Yes, Bob's done very well, and I'm sure he's going right to the top."

"It's hard work and long hours and now there's this case. . . ."

"Desmond Barlow. Yes, it's an unpleasant one."

"Yes, well, I used to see him at the day center — he was one of the helpers. A real old-fashioned do-gooder, if you know what I mean; always knew what was best for you. Most of the helpers, the volunteers, were really nice, kind and friendly, but he was — what would you call it? — patronizing. I thought to myself, 'You'll be old yourself one day and then you'll know what it's like.'"

"I do know what you mean about patronizing," I said. "I expect Bob's told you that I do a few days at the charity shop that Desmond runs — used to run — and we all felt the same as you did. Not a nice man."

"And now poor Bob's got to find out who killed him. You'll be spoiled for choice, I told him. Everyone disliked him."

"But, I suppose, not enough to kill him!"

"No, that's what Bob said. But you know, there was something a bit fishy about him."

"Really?"

"Well, I'll tell you. My next-door neighbor takes me to the garden center sometimes, when he's going himself. I like to have a bit of a look round, and we usually have a cup of coffee in the café there — it makes a nice morning out. Well, anyway, I needed some special plant food for my fuchsia and some more compost. Dave, that's my friend, was off outside looking at fruit trees — he wants to do a cordoned pear — and I was in that side bit where they have the packets and bottles of stuff — did you know you can't buy Bordeaux mixture anymore? Something to do with the Common Market. A lot of stupid nonsense! Like I was saying, I like to look round there — it's usually nice and quiet. The main part's always crowded and I do find it a bit difficult with my walking frame. Anyway, I turned the corner and who should I see but that Desmond Barlow talking to another man — very spruce in a city suit. It looked like they were arguing, quite heated. When they saw me they stopped, and Mr. Barlow, he recognized me and gave me *such* a look! Well, if looks could kill!"

"Good gracious. What did you do?"

"Went and got my plant food, while they stood there and watched me. Well, I'd got as much right to be there as them — more, if you ask me. It didn't look like they were there to buy anything."

"Really?"

"Didn't seem to have been looking at the stuff there."

"You mean they were there because it was a quiet place where they could discuss something?"

"That's right. The other man, the one in a suit, he didn't look as if *he* was a gardener!"

"So when you'd got your plant food — incidentally, you must tell me the name of it; my fuchsias could do with a bit of a boost — what happened then?"

"Like I said, they just stood there and waited for me to go. I didn't let on I recognized Mr. Barlow — I wasn't going to give him that satisfaction. And I took my time leaving. Well, I can't move too quickly with my walking frame. They weren't too happy about it."

I laughed. "Well done," I said. "But what an extraordinary thing. I don't suppose you happened to hear anything they were saying."

"Mr. Barlow was saying something about it being the other man's responsibility, and *he* said something like 'You don't get out of it like that,' and then they saw me and shut up."

"That's very interesting," I said thoughtfully.

"I saw the other man leaving," Reg said, "when we were going into the café. He got into a big posh car and drove off in a hurry. He didn't look as if he was from around here — a London type, if you ask me."

"Did you tell Bob about all this?" I asked.

"You mean it might have something to do with this case he's so busy with?"

"Well, you think yourself it was all a bit odd, so it might be. It could be very helpful."

"I might do that, then. He says he's dropping in this evening. I'll tell him then and say you think it might be important."

Bob phoned me the next day.

"Thanks for going to see Dad. He really enjoyed seeing you. And thanks for getting him to tell me about that man George Arnold; it certainly seems worth following up."

"I must say I thought it was a bit suspicious, the way he spoke to Wendy and offered to sort through Desmond's business papers."

"Yes, I think we might have a look at them — I don't suppose Mrs. Barlow would object."

"Wendy? No, she's much too occupied with selling the house and moving to Birmingham with her son."

"Moving, did you say?" Bob said sharply.

"Yes — I don't suppose she thought to tell you. She's very vague. But now John's going to the art school there, she says there's nothing to keep her in Taviscombe.

They lived in Birmingham for a while when Desmond was working in the area, and she may still know people there."

"I'd rather she didn't leave Taviscombe while the case is still in progress."

"Can you stop her leaving? Surely you don't think she's a suspect."

"There are still a number of questions I need to ask her. And her son."

"I see. Well, I expect it'll take some time to sell the house — this is always a bad time of the year to sell, isn't it — so she'll be around for a while yet."

There was a pause. Then Bob said: "I'm surprised she didn't tell me she was going to leave Taviscombe. I would have thought she might have been interested to know who killed her husband," he added with heavy irony.

"Oh dear, yes, you would think so, wouldn't you. But the fact is that Wendy, while not wishing her husband any ill, is more relieved than sad to be rid of him. And no, I don't believe for a moment that she had anything to do with his death. It's just that she's been living all these years with a thoroughly disagreeable man who bullied and dominated her, made her life pretty miserable and his son's life so wretched that he was going to run away. So it's not

148

surprising that she's relieved and, yes, happy to be free of him."

"But surely . . ."

"She seems to have put it all behind her, as if it was another life — as, I suppose it is, to her now. She's a very naive person. I imagine that's how she came to marry Desmond; she took him at his face value. He, of course, married her for her money. As I say, she's very naive, took life as it came, became a doormat to her husband. The only time she ever rebelled (if you can call it that) was over her son, and even there she was never brave enough to speak out, only tried to make things easier for John by concealing things from Desmond. But now it's all over, as she sees it, she's moved on so thoroughly that I don't believe she gives a thought as to *how* he died or who killed him. It's all like another life to her. She just wants to begin her new life. Now."

There was a long pause while Bob tried to take in a concept he found hard to accept. Then he said, "You really think that's the way she is; she's not just putting on an act?"

"I'm sure of it. I knew her when Desmond was alive; I saw how it was. Like you, I couldn't believe she could be so — well — detached. But she is — I do really believe it."

Another pause. "Well, what do they say? 'There's nowt so queer as folk!' "

I laughed. "It took me a while to get used to it, especially since, as I said, I've seen her with Desmond, like a frightened rabbit."

"Anyway, you've given me quite a lot to think about. There are still several things I want to ask her, but I'll bear in mind what you've told me when I do."

"You must form your own opinion, of course. I'll be interested to know what you think."

"Right. I'll be in touch. And I'll let you know what, if anything, I find in those business papers." He laughed. "I think I'll feel on firmer ground with them, more what I'm used to!"

Whenever I go to pick up Alice from her ballet class I always have a strong sense of *déja vu.* In these very rooms I had, at that same barre, hesitantly gone up on my pointes, practiced my pliés and finally achieved a rather wobbly arabesque, while Madam (Josie Blackwood from Porlock) had continued her endless argument with the pianist (whose name I have now forgotten) about the tempo. The notes of what was probably that same piano greeted me when I joined the group of mothers (and grandmothers) waiting, just inside the door, to collect their budding ballerinas. There was a low murmur of conversation ("What with piano lessons and swimming and now ballet, I spend all my time driving the twins around. And the expense!"), but their eyes followed the movements of their offspring with satisfaction ("Flora is dancing with the older girls in the display this year; Madam says she's come along so well."). Josie, of course, is long gone, but Maisie Fletcher carries on the tradition, and so there is still a Madam.

To my surprise I saw that the pianist was Margaret Curtis When the class was over I went over to have a word with her.

"Hello, Margaret. I never knew you had this hidden talent — so clever. Playing for dancing must be very tricky!"

She looked pleased at this mild praise. "Oh, I don't know. I love playing and Maisie needed someone when Brenda could only come part-time, so I'm filling in for her. I come on the days when I'm not at the shop. I like to be busy, and it's lovely to see all the children."

"Well, good for you." I looked around the room. "Goodness, how it all takes me back! I used to come to ballet classes here well over fifty years ago. Nothing seems to have changed, except that your playing is so much better than the pianist then. Gladys Middleton!" I brought the name out triumphantly. "A disagreeable woman, very bad tempered, with a perpetual cold."

Margaret laughed. "It's funny, isn't it, how vivid childhood memories are. While I can hardly remember what happened last week, I can still remember every detail about my first music teacher. She was very strict, picked you up on every tiny fault, but she was a wonderful teacher and a single word of praise from her was something you really worked for!"

"Well, it's certainly paid off for you. But I'd better go," I said, conscious that Alice was hopping up and down with barely contained impatience. "My granddaughter seems to want to tell me something."

Alice grabbed my arm and almost pulled me out of the room. "Gran, Gran, Madam says I can dance one of the fairies in the end-of-term display. She only chose four of us; she said we were the best. Mummy has to make me a costume. We're all different colors — I'm blue — and we're going to have *wings*, you know, fastened to our wrists so we can flutter." She waved her arms up and down. "Like this."

"Lovely, darling. We'll all be very proud."

"I *love* ballet. Not as much as riding — I'm better at that — but it's such fun and, besides, Hannah does ballet." Hannah was Alice's new best friend. "She's very good. Madam thinks she might be ready to go up on her pointes quite soon. Isn't that exciting?"

"Very exciting. Now, do get into the car. Mummy will have tea ready."

"I have to go out," Norma said, "so I'll leave you to hold the fort." She glanced out of the window at the driving rain. "I don't expect you'll be very busy." She picked up her umbrella and departed.

"Gone to have coffee with her friend from Malvern," Jean said sourly. "Well, she's not the only one who wants coffee. I'll go and make some for us." She appeared soon after with mugs of coffee and a tin of biscuits. "Her ladyship's special chocolate digestives. Here, help yourself. I'd better put the tin back."

Norma was right about not being busy. We sipped our coffee and ate our biscuits while we watched passersby with their heads down hurrying past, only concerned with getting in out of the rain, certainly unwilling to stop and look in our window.

"I didn't know that Margaret played the

153

piano for Maisie Fletcher's dance class," I said idly. "I saw her there when I went to pick up my granddaughter."

"Oh, she's a very good pianist. Not concert standard, of course, but very good. I think she's glad of the extra money."

"Really?"

"Well, you know she retired early from her teaching job — some sort of sinus trouble — so her pension isn't that much, and I think she finds it difficult to make ends meet. She used to give music lessons, but they sort of tailed off. Well, people don't have the money these days, do they?"

"I'm so sorry. I hadn't realized."

"Oh, Margaret's a great one for keeping up appearances. And, of course, she's still in that old cottage where she used to live with her mother. I believe *she* contributed a bit to the upkeep, but when she died I think Margaret's found it difficult. Well, you know how these old places always need *something* doing to them."

"Only too well!"

"But, like she said, it's her only asset so she has to keep it in good order. I mean she might have to sell it if she has to go into a home or anything."

"I suppose so. Poor soul, it must be such a worry."

"It certainly is. She told me —" Jean broke off and lowered her voice. "I shouldn't be telling you this, but I know you won't let it go any further. She was desperate for money, to do with the wiring of the cottage. I don't know the details, but it was something that *had* to be done. Well, she happened to be in the shop on her own when some china came in, a whole box of it. She was just putting it in the back to be looked at when one of our experts came, when she noticed one piece. A vase, nothing much to look at — you wouldn't get more than 60p for it — but Margaret had seen one just like it on one of those antiques programs on TV, worth hundreds."

"Good heavens!"

"The same mark on the bottom and everything. Well, she was desperate, like I say, and she says she just gave in to temptation. She hid it outside in the shed with all the books to go for salvage, so that she could find out what it would go for at auction. Mind you, you never do get what they say, do you? And then there's the auction fee. Anyway, to cut a long story short, Desmond found it."

"Oh dear!"

"The trouble was, he knew that Margaret had unpacked that box."

"So what happened?"

"He confronted her with it. Very unpleasant, you know what he was like. Said he ought to call the police."

"No!"

"He laid it on very thick. Said they'd take a very dim view because she was defrauding a charity. She begged him not to, of course, but he went on at great length. Finally he said he hadn't made up his mind what to do and he'd think about it and let her know. Oh, he was enjoying it, all right. You know how he liked to have a hold over people."

"When was this?"

"Quite a while ago. She asked him several times what he'd decided but he kept on saying he hadn't made up his mind."

"How vile!"

"She told me about it one day — I think she had to talk to someone. She said that, anyway, when she'd thought about it, she'd already decided not to go through with it after all, not to take the vase. She was at the end of her tether, I can tell you, and I do believe she was on the point of going to the police herself when, luckily for her, Desmond died and she was able to breathe again."

CHAPTER ELEVEN

Jean's last words hung in the air, and for a minute we were both silent. Then Jean said, "Of course, I never meant to suggest that Margaret . . ."

"Good heavens, no."

"The *last* person."

"Absolutely."

"Mind you," Jean said, "if Desmond behaved like that to Margaret, goodness knows what he might have done to someone else. I mean, there might have been something really serious, so that whoever it was felt they had to kill him to stop him saying anything."

I thought of George Arnold. "That's true," I said. "After all, we don't know that much about Desmond; he hadn't been in Taviscombe very long."

"You're right. How do we know what he was up to before he came here!"

I think we both felt that it was comforting

somehow, the thought that whatever caused the murder, and whoever did it, was from the past and from somewhere else.

The sound of Norma opening the shop door and shaking her wet umbrella outside broke up our conversation. Jean snatched up the mugs and disappeared into the storeroom, and I hastily picked up a duster and began polishing the counter.

"Oh, Sheila." Anthea accosted me as soon as I entered Brunswick Lodge. "I was just going to ring you."

"Yes?" I said warily.

"It's about this book sale."

"What book sale?"

"The one on the nineteenth. It was all decided at the last committee meeting — the one you didn't come to."

"No, I explained to George — I'd arranged to babysit that evening."

"Yes, well, the sale is going ahead, and we all agreed that since you know all about books, you should be in charge."

"But I won't be here on the nineteenth," I protested. "That's a Saturday and Thea's got tickets for all of us to go to the matinee in Bristol. I can't possibly cancel that."

"Well," Anthea said grudgingly. "I don't suppose it matters if you're not here for the sale — anyone can do the actual selling. No, what we want you to do is go through the books people bring in and price them."

"Oh, I can do that," I said, relieved to have got off relatively lightly.

"We've had a very good response so far, though, of course, those charity shops of yours have taken a lot of the ones we might have had."

"When do you want me to come?" I asked, refusing to take responsibility for all the charity shops in Taviscombe.

"I'd think next Monday would be all right; we should have quite a few books by then. And bring in as many books as you can from people you know. Not those literary things of yours — no one will want *them*."

"I'll see what I can find," I said cautiously.

The books were neatly stacked up in the small committee room. I was pleased to see that the heating had been put on and thought more kindly of Anthea for thinking of it. I was crouched down on the floor examining the books when Marcus Stanley came in.

"Oh good," he said. "It's warmed up nicely — that's really quite a good heater."

I got awkwardly to my feet and he said, "I'll just put the books on the table so we can get at them."

"Anthea didn't say you'd be helping," I said. Then, thinking that sounded a little ungrateful, I added, "It's very good of you."

"Norma thought you might need a hand."

"Oh. Oh, I see. Well, thank you very much."

"Such a good idea, this book sale," he said. "Norma suggested it and the committee were very keen. As Norma says, I'm sure we all have books on our shelves we hardly ever read."

"I have many books on my shelves that I hardly ever read," I protested, "and it's so delightful when you suddenly come across an old friend you haven't looked at for ages. No, I find it very difficult to get rid of any book, however little I may read it."

"But surely paperbacks?"

"Some of my greatest treasures are paperbacks. I still have some of those old Penguins with orange covers and detective novels with green ones. It gives me so much pleasure to remember how I saved up for them when I was young and where I bought them and who with."

"You must have a lot of books," Marcus said respectfully.

"Bookshelves in every room," I said proudly. "No space for any more, so the books are mostly double stacked — almost impossible to find anything. Michael says they're the only thing holding the cottage together — if we took them down the whole place would collapse." He laughed politely. "Still," I said, "I did manage to find a few books — mostly things people thought I *ought* to read — as my contribution."

I sat down at the table and pulled a pile of books towards me. "Right, then," I said. "Shall I do the hardbacks while you do the paperbacks?"

He hesitated. "To be honest," he said, "I wouldn't have the faintest idea what to charge."

"Oh."

It became obvious to me that Norma had sent Marcus along (presumably without Anthea's knowledge) as her representative, to stake her claim, as it were, on Anthea's territory.

"I could make us some coffee," Marcus suggested.

"That would be marvelous," I said. "Thank you so much."

When he came back with the coffee, in cups not mugs, with separate milk and sugar and some biscuits on a plate — Norma had trained him well — I'd marked up quite a few of the books.

"Some quite good things here," I said as I cleared a space on the table for the tray. "No valuable first editions, alas, but lots of interesting stuff. Several I'd quite like myself; I daresay I could squeeze in a couple more volumes."

I poured some milk into my coffee and took a biscuit, and Marcus did the same and sat down at the table opposite to me.

"How do you like living down here?" I asked.

"Oh, I've always loved it. My parents spent a lot of time abroad. My father had business interests in the Middle East. I was at boarding school so I spent most of the holidays here with my aunt. I always thought of it as my home. When I was at Oxford, though, my parents settled back in England so I didn't come down here as much."

"What was your aunt's name? I wonder if I knew her."

"My mother's sister, her name was Seaton. Edith Seaton."

I thought for a moment. "Oh yes," I said. "My mother knew her slightly. They used to play bridge together occasionally."

"She was a great bridge player," Marcus said. "She tried to teach me to play, but I never really got the hang of it."

"Oh, I know what you mean. I've never

been any good at card games. Not that you can call bridge a card game, more of a religion. Your aunt died quite recently, then?"

"Yes. She left the house to me because I was her last living relative — though I think she was fond of me as well. She was rather an austere sort of person — it was hard to tell what she felt."

"And did you and Norma come down quite often after you were married?"

He hesitated. "My work was rather demanding. It was difficult to get away, so we didn't get down as often as I would have liked. And Norma had so many interests. . . ."

"Of course. Still, it's nice that you've finally come home, as you might say. As I recall, it's a big house with a lot of ground."

"Yes. We had to have a great deal done to it before we moved in. My aunt had rather let things go — you know how old people don't care to have things changed. Norma said it was like living in a time warp, everything so old-fashioned. The kitchen and bathroom had to be completely remodeled and everywhere else redecorated. The grounds were well kept — my aunt had two gardeners — but Norma has got a garden designer in and she's having a tennis court laid out and possibly a swimming pool. She's very keen that we should take plenty of exercise."

"Goodness. What energy! All that and what she does here, at Brunswick Lodge, not to mention the charity shop. I don't know how she fits it all in."

"She's very well organized."

"Oh yes, I've noticed that at the shop. I suppose that's why she was at odds with Desmond."

"I wouldn't say that exactly."

"Well, you know what I mean. Two strong-minded people, each with clear ideas of how things should be done. But, of course, Desmond was a very difficult person, not just to work with but in every way. I think we all had our problems with him. He must have made lots of enemies, don't you think?"

"I didn't really know him. I used to see him briefly when I went into the shop, but we never saw him socially."

"No, nor did I." He nodded. "But it was such a dreadful thing," I went on, "his dying like that. . . . We were all so shocked. We couldn't believe how something like that could have happened."

"Norma was very upset."

He was obviously disinclined to say more, probably because of the delicate situation between Norma and Desmond. "Anyway," I said, "things are certainly running very smoothly now Norma's in charge."

He looked pleased. "She does seem to have a gift for that kind of thing. I believe they're going to put her in charge — officially, that is — though nothing's been confirmed yet."

"That's good," I said, putting my cup on the tray. "Well, we'd better get on. Could you sort out those paperbacks into piles: detective fiction, other fiction and nonfiction? Oh, and there's a good lot of Mills and Boone. They always go well; put them in a separate pile."

Just then the door opened and Norma came in. For a moment she looked disconcerted at the cozy scene — the tray with the cups and plates, the gas fire casting a warm glow and Marcus and I seated at the table obviously chatting and not suitably employed.

Marcus got to his feet and looked flustered. Norma ignored him and said, "I just looked in to see how you're getting on."

"Oh, splendidly," I said airily. "I've nearly finished the hardbacks, and Marcus is just going to sort out the paperbacks into categories."

"Excellent," Norma said graciously. She

came forward and picked up the tray. "I'll just take this out of the way to make more room for you," she said and went out, not quite shutting the door behind her. I wondered if she'd left it open on purpose in case we made any remark after she'd left. But I just smiled at Marcus, who smiled, rather hesitantly, back.

"You might find it easier to sort those paperbacks into piles on the floor," I said. "If you don't mind. And I'll carry on here."

We worked on in silence for a while, both rather expecting another visit, and indeed there was. This time it was Anthea.

"Nobody told me that Marcus was coming," she began.

"Yes, wasn't it kind of him?" I said. "It's been such a help. There now, I've finished these, so, Marcus, if you could take them and put them on that broad windowsill over there and arrange them in alphabetical order by author. And if you just bring me those separate piles of paperbacks, I can get on with those — that's right, thank you so much."

I often find the best way to cope with Anthea is simply to talk right over her. It always throws her and it sometimes shuts her up.

"Well, I'll leave you to it," she said grudgingly and went off, presumably to find Norma and "have it out" with her.

Once again I smiled at Marcus, and this time his smile was almost a grin.

"He really is quite nice," I said to Rosemary, "when you get him on his own and when he's not banging on about Norma. I think if it hadn't been suppressed by her, he might have had a perfectly good sense of humor."

"Poor thing."

"And his childhood sounds pretty miserable. Parents abroad, boarding school from very young and holidays with that dismal aunt — you remember old Mrs. Seaton."

"Yes, Mother knew her for a bit, but she couldn't be doing with all that bridge. Pots of money and lived alone in that enormous house, very straitlaced and forbidding. It can't have been much fun for poor little Marcus."

"Yet he spoke about the holidays (well, about being down here) with great affection. I suppose it was the only sort of home life, if you can call that home life, he knew. I expect that's why he married Norma, to have a family of his own — though there don't seem to have been any children."

"Just as well; think of having Norma for a

mother! And she presumably grabbed him because of the money. Do we know where it came from?"

"He said something about his parents having business interests in the Middle East, so perhaps he went into the family firm. And he said something about his work being very demanding so that he couldn't get down here very often. But I think it's most likely that Norma didn't get on with his aunt and he thought it was better to keep them apart."

"Especially if he was going to inherit! Have you seen the house now that Norma's given it a makeover?"

"No. I think they give select little dinner parties for the great and the good of Taviscombe, to which, naturally, we peasants are not invited. She's on more committees than I ever knew existed. The money helps, of course, but she's managed to bulldoze her way into every level of what you might call Taviscombe society!"

Rosemary laughed. "Oh, the horror of it!"

"She's getting really sure of herself now; not so long ago she trod more cautiously. She wasn't quite sure how to handle Desmond; she kept quiet far more often then than she would now. I think it really rankled with her that she couldn't get the better of him at the shop. They were both bullies, and I must say it was great fun to see them walking round each other like that. If things had gone on I think there'd have been an almighty bust-up. But, of course, now Desmond is no more, she's queen bee at last."

"Hmm," Rosemary said thoughtfully. "A good reason to get rid of him, do you think?"

"Murder? Norma? Not very likely — I'm sure she'd have got the upper hand some other way. Besides, she went home early with a migraine that day."

"Oh, come on! Nothing's easier to fake than a migraine. She could easily have come back later and done the deed. I'm sure the wretched Marcus would have given her an alibi if asked."

"True. And come to think of it, I thought at the time her going home was more because of a huff than a migraine. But, really, I don't think it's Norma's style. She's so sure of getting her own way eventually that she wouldn't think it necessary!"

"That's as may be," Rosemary said, "but I'll still think of her as a likely suspect. Oh, by the way, what I wanted to ask you — and with all this Marcus thing I forgot — would you be an angel and come to Taunton with me on Monday? Mother wants me to get her a couple of new nightdresses, and I know she'll hate everything I bring back, but if I say you chose them then she might — just might — approve. I tried to suggest she should order something from a catalog, but she says catalogs are 'common,' even the very superior ones. So do say you'll come. I'll stand you lunch at the new place in the Precinct."

I ran into Bob Morris in the library, in the gardening section. He looked up when I greeted him.

"My dad wants a book on tomatoes. I don't think there's much here. I did offer to buy one for him, but he said it might not tell him what he wanted to know and would be a waste of money."

I smiled. "Very sensible. How is he?"

Bob shook his head. "Not very happy. This damp weather doesn't do his hip any good."

"Such a pity he won't have the operation," I said.

"Betty and me, we're still trying to persuade him, but you know what it's like."

"We all get more obstinate as we get older. Anyway," I said, "how are things going with the case?"

"Not very well, as a matter of fact. I've been trying to chase up stuff about George

Arnold. I wanted to check through Desmond Barlow's business papers before he gets to look at them."

"But?"

"But I can't get hold of Mrs. Barlow. I've called around a couple of times and phoned repeatedly, but she doesn't seem to be there. It looks as though she's gone away.

"I wouldn't have thought that was very likely," I said thoughtfully.

"I did ask her not to leave Taviscombe, but she didn't seem to take much notice."

"No, I wouldn't have thought she'd go away and leave Tiger."

"Tiger?"

"Her cat."

"Well, it's all a great nuisance. Oh well, I've got a few other lines of inquiry to follow up, so I'll have to get on with them. There's still the theft of the money from the till — we haven't got far with that." He paused. "You know how it is, when you feel that whichever way you turn you've finished up in a dead end!"

"I'm sure you'll get a breakthrough soon," I said comfortingly. "Meanwhile," I said, plucking a book from the shelves, "how would this one do? *The Complete Tomato Handbook.* He can't say what he wants isn't in this!"

CHAPTER TWELVE

We caught a fairly early train to Bristol. Thea and I were taking Alice and her friend Hannah to see their first proper ballet — *The Nutcracker,* of course. The matinee wasn't until two thirty, but Alice was determined to squeeze every last drop of entertainment out of the day and had insisted we should have pizzas at a special place that Hannah had once been to with her parents. The theater was full of little girls, many of whom had persuaded their mothers to let them come in their tutus, something Alice and Hannah obviously regarded with disapproval as babyish. But as they sat, leaning forward, their eyes shining, the bags of sweets forgotten on their laps, they too were completely lost in the magic.

We came out into the real world, all of us still half dazed by the swirl of the music in our heads and the colorfulness of the settings and the costumes still vividly before our eyes. It was a particular shock, therefore, to be nearly knocked over by a couple young people rushing past, almost pushing us off the pavement. They were a disreputable-looking pair, scruffily dressed, who looked as if they'd been sleeping rough. The boy was tall and loutish and seemed to be arguing with the girl whom he had by the wrist, pulling her along after him. She was very thin and, from what I could see of the expression on her face half hidden by the tangled hair, she was reluctant to go with him. Although there was no actual violence, it was a disagreeable moment, made worse by the fact that the girls were upset and a little frightened.

"For goodness' sake!" Thea cried after the couple. "What do you think you're doing!"

But they'd gone, turned down a side alley, and we were left feeling furious and frustrated. The contrast between the fairy world of the ballet and harsh reality was particularly distressing. Fortunately I saw a taxi approaching, hailed it and bundled the others in.

"We'll have a drink and something to eat at the station," I said. "Is that all right?"

Thea nodded gratefully and the girls, diverted by riding in a taxi (a novelty for children usually driven about in cars),

173

seemed enthusiastic.

"Can we have hot chocolate?" Alice asked.

"I don't know if they have it," I said. "But if they do, you can."

In the train, the girls, who seemed to have shrugged off what had been a nasty experience, had got out their programs and were living the magic again.

"That tree! The way it suddenly *grew*!"

"Those mice!"

"The snowflakes and the flowers!"

"And the dresses!"

Thea and I sat back in our seats, watching them affectionately but really too tired to say anything. I was thinking about the unpleasant incident, grateful for the resilience of children. Something was nagging at me — something at the back of my mind wanted my attention.

"Of course," I said out loud. "Sophie Randall!"

"Sophie Randall?" Thea echoed. "What about her?"

"That girl. I only got a glimpse of her face, but I'm sure that's who it was."

"I didn't really see her," Thea said. "I was hanging on to the children in case they got pushed into the road — all that traffic!"

"I'm sure it was her."

"I wouldn't be surprised. She's very wild,

I believe."

"Gran," Alice said, looking up from her program. "Hannah's going to be a ballerina when she grows up." Alice seemed to have established herself as the means of communication between her friend (a silent girl who rarely expressed an opinion) and the adult world. "Because she's good at ballet. Madam says so. I'm not good enough — you have to be super good to be a real ballerina — but I'm going to do all the costumes and the scenery because I'm good at drawing and painting."

"That's nice," I said.

I told Rosemary about Sophie Randall when we happened to meet in the Buttery next day.

"I can't say I'm surprised," she said. "She went off to Bristol last time when she was living in that squat."

"Have her parents heard from her?"

"I wouldn't think so — she never contacted them before."

"Do you think I ought to let them know? I mean, they must be desperately worried. I'm really positive it was her. The thing is, I don't really know them — I mean, I wouldn't want them to think I'm interfering."

"I'm sure they'd want to know — *we* would!"

"Well, of course."

"I'll ring Mrs. Randall if you like. I've got her number because she once asked me if I could pick up Daisy from school when I fetched Delia. Then she can ring you if she wants to know any more."

"Oh, would you? That would be the best thing. Thinking about it, I'm really worried about the poor girl. She looked dreadful, and I didn't like the way that awful young man was dragging her along like that."

"The poor Randalls," Rosemary said soberly. "You try to bring your children up properly, you give them love and security and then something like this happens. It doesn't seem fair."

"We've been lucky," I said. "So far."

"So far," Rosemary echoed. We were silent for a minute; then Rosemary went on: "At least if the Randalls know she's in Bristol, they may be able to find her — that's something. Come on, let's have another Danish pastry to cheer ourselves up."

Next day I asked Jean when she'd last seen Sophie in the shop.

"Goodness, I don't know." She thought for a moment. "Just before Desmond died,

I think." I noticed how we all used the word "died" about Desmond — "killed" or "murdered" was too explicit.

"Come to think of it, she was hanging around here the day before. I remember now; Norma spoke quite sharply to her and Sophie was very rude to her." She laughed. "She used language I don't suppose Norma had ever heard before. Why do you want to know?"

I explained how I'd seen her in Bristol and was worried about her.

"What can you do!" she said. "Young people nowadays — no idea how to behave, no respect for anyone or anything."

"Not all of them!" I protested.

"Well, perhaps not all, but when I think of what this town used to be like — you'll remember it, too. And now there's drugs — in a small town like Taviscombe! — and young people drunk in the streets. . . ." She shook her head. "That Sophie always looked such a mess, her face pierced like that, and I'm sure she never took a brush to her hair. She could have been such a pretty girl. I mean, you're only young once, aren't you, and it doesn't last that long, the chance to look nice and wear pretty clothes. Such a waste."

"Well," I said. "Now her parents know

where she is. I hope they'll be able to find her and bring her back."

I was still thinking about Sophie when I got home, and it suddenly occurred to me that she might well have been the person who took the money from the till the night Desmond was killed. While I was cooking some fish for the animals, I decided that I really ought to let Bob Morris know what I thought. He was discreet and would question the Randalls tactfully — they might, anyway, have already reported her as a missing person. But it would be helpful to know when she ran off to Bristol. And if she had been in the shop, it would be important to know what time. In fact, it suddenly seemed urgent that I should ring him right away. Leaving the fish in the microwave, where Foss couldn't get at it, I rang the police station, only to be told that Bob Morris was out of the station for the day and would ring me in the morning.

But having got this idea into my head I was very restless and cast around for something I could do about it. The only thing I could think of was to phone Rosemary.

"Yes, I did phone Mrs. Randall and she was very grateful; they'd already been to the squat in Bristol where Sophie was before, but there was no sign of her and no one there knew where she was — at least they said they didn't. But she said at least now they know that Sophie's still in Bristol. I didn't tell her about the man dragging her along — I thought it would upset her. I just said she was with a young man. I suppose he was the one she was going around with here. You didn't recognize him, I suppose?"

"No, it all happened so fast. But I am going to tell Bob Morris about it." I told her my theory about Sophie having taken the money and she agreed it was very likely.

"Oh dear, the poor Randalls! There seems to be no end to it. Awful for Daisy, too. She's just at that age. . . ."

"Let's hope what's happened to Sophie will keep her on the straight and narrow."

The next morning I still couldn't get hold of Bob Morris. But as I was driving past the end of Wendy Barlow's road, I thought I'd go and see if there was any sign of her. The house had that shut-up look homes develop when they've been empty for a little while. Still, I rang the bell and went round to the side gate, which was, of course, locked. I was trying to peer in through the front room window when a voice behind me said, "She's away."

I turned round in some embarrassment and saw a woman who had just emerged from the house next door. She had her coat on and a shopping bag in her hand.

"Oh — yes — I just wanted a word. I work in the charity shop with her," I said hastily, wanting to establish my credentials. "We were trying to get in touch with her — about coming in — she hasn't been answering her phone and, of course, after what's happened, we did worry — not that there was any reason to, I'm sure — but you never know, do you. . . ."

I'd made my way to the front gate, and she came forward to meet me.

"No, she went away a while back," she said. "Canceled the milk, the milkman told me — left a note — till further notice."

"Goodness!" I said. "It must have been sudden — I mean, she didn't let us know and she's usually very reliable. Still, I suppose now . . ."

"That's right. Not herself at all, poor soul. Well, you can't wonder at it. Such a dreadful thing." I noted with satisfaction the sudden animation in her voice. "You wouldn't believe such a thing could happen, not here, not in Taviscombe! Mind you" — she came nearer — "I never liked him. Not a nice man at all. He was very unpleasant about our fence, *and* most unhelpful about that tree — completely overshadowed our rose bed. Too fond of his own opinion, if you know what I mean. And that poor little woman, couldn't call her soul her own. If you ask me, it was a merciful release for her, and for the son, though he was a bit of a drip, as my husband used to say. Still, you wouldn't be surprised, would you, with a father like that."

"I wonder when she's coming back," I said. "And what about the cat?" I asked suddenly.

"Oh, that cat! Quite soft about it, she was, but then, she'd never had an animal before, poor thing. I couldn't live without my Charlie — he's a spaniel, getting on a bit now. . . ."

"They're lovely, aren't they? So affectionate. But what about the cat?"

"Oh, she had it in a cat box — saw her loading up the car and went out to have a word with her. Well, you need to know if your neighbors are going away, don't you, leaving the house empty, especially nowadays. No, she had quite a lot of stuff in boxes and a couple of suitcases. Filled up the boot. The cat box was in the car — such a racket the animal was making. As a matter of fact I only had a few words with her

— said she was going away and would I keep an eye on things — but before I'd had a chance to ask her where she was going and for how long, she was distracted by that cat and said she had to go."

"Well, that is inconvenient," I said. "It doesn't look as if she's coming back to the shop, but I do wish she'd told us. We'll have to try and find someone to replace her. It's the holiday season and we're always busy then, so we do need a full staff."

"Yes, there's a lot of tourists about — everywhere gets very crowded."

"Well," I said, "I mustn't hold you up — you've been most helpful." I looked at her shopping bag. "Can I give you a lift anywhere?"

"No, thanks. I only want a few things so I'm just going to the shops in the Parade — not worth getting the car out. And I always say a nice walk does you a lot of good."

Now more than ever I wanted to get hold of Bob Morris to tell him about Wendy as well as my news about Sophie. I felt her going away must have had something to do with John. Could she have gone to Birmingham with him, and would she ever come back? The fact that she'd taken Tiger with her did indicate that she was planning to be away for some time. As she was now, I don't suppose she even thought about letting the police know that she was going or leaving them her address. As Bob had said, she didn't seem to care about her husband's murder — too excited, I suppose, about her new life. Extraordinary. Presumably the college of art in Birmingham would have an address for John and Bob could trace her through him. Not that I thought she had anything to do with Desmond's murder, but still . . .

Foss's insistent demand for food made me think about Tiger. His comfort would be a major concern for her, so she wasn't likely to take him with her to a hotel and she certainly wouldn't have put him in a cattery. Tris now joined Foss, adding short peremptory barks to the Siamese wailing. To pacify them I uncovered the remains of the fish and fed them. In the blissful silence that ensued the phone rang. It was Bob Morris.

"Sorry I was out when you rang."

"I've got some news for you," I said. "Two pieces of news, actually."

"And I have news for you. The Randalls have had a call from the Royal Infirmary in Bristol. Their daughter Sophie is in there.

She's taken an overdose and they don't know if they can save her."

CHAPTER THIRTEEN

For a moment I couldn't take in what Bob was saying. I'd seen Sophie so recently; it seemed impossible she should be close to death.

"That's terrible," I said. "One of the things I was going to tell you was that I saw her in Bristol last Saturday. I thought she might have been the person who took the money from the till. . . ." My voice trailed away. Somehow it seemed wrong to be thinking of it now.

"That was something I'd been following up," Bob said. "Her parents had reported her missing the day after Desmond Barlow was killed, so it seemed there might be a link. Anyway, the hospital phoned them last night and they went there straightaway."

"Poor souls — they've had a horrible time. What sort of overdose? Did she take it herself, or was it accidental?"

"I don't know the details yet."

"No, of course not."

"I had thought," he went on, "that if we could find her and she *was* the one who took the money, then she might be able to fix the time of the murder. But now, of course . . . The hospital will let me know how things are going."

"Yes. We must just hope she recovers — for everyone's sake. They can do such wonderful things now. I'm sure they can save her."

We were both silent for a moment. There seemed nothing else we could say. Then Bob said, "There were two things you were going to tell me."

"Oh yes — though it hardly seems important after all this." I told him about my visit to Wendy's house and what her neighbor had said. "It sounds as if she's planning to stay away for quite a while, though she'll have to come back to see to the house — if she's going to sell it, that is."

"And you think she's gone to Birmingham?" Bob asked.

"That seems most likely. I know it's maddening that she's gone, but she has made a statement; do you need to see her again?"

"Even though we don't know the exact time of death, it seems that neither Mrs. Barlow or her son had any sort of alibi for the whole evening. And quite frankly, from what I've been able to find out, they were the ones who had the strongest motive for murder."

"I suppose so."

"Mrs. Malory," Bob began. He paused, then went on. "Mrs. Malory, I know you think she couldn't have killed her husband. Obviously you know her better than I do and have had more of a chance to, well, sum up her character. You may well be right and, of course, I do consider all that very carefully. I really appreciate all you've done and found out — things I probably couldn't have found out as you did. But, when all's said and done, I have to work with the facts. That's my job."

"Of *course* it is," I said. "I'm sorry. I do get carried away sometimes. It's very good of you to let me know what's happening. I do appreciate it."

"And I appreciate all you've done to help. Like I said, you've been able to get people to talk in a way I never could and I hope you'll go on doing it, but the bottom line is getting the *evidence,* all the boring, plodding bit — well, I'm sure I don't have to tell you that!"

"Of course," I repeated. "And I do realize you can't let Wendy just disappear. I suppose you could get an address for John from the college of art. She's bound to be with him."

"Yes, I'll get onto that right away. And I'll let you know," he said, "what news there is about Sophie Randall."

I put the receiver down with mixed feelings. I'd been put in my place — in the nicest possible way — by Bob Morris, and he'd been right to do so. I was only an inquisitive amateur; he was the professional. It was (as he reminded me) his job. And he was good at it. He'd been very polite, grateful for my help, and had promised to keep me in touch with his investigations, but I realized that my relationship with him was quite different from the one I'd had with Roger Eliot when he was investigating things. Roger was Rosemary's son-in-law, the husband of my goddaughter Jilly — of course it was different.

"I felt — not embarrassed exactly, *disconcerted,* I suppose," I said to Rosemary when I rang her, as I always do when I have a problem. "Awkward, really. I'm not sure now how much I can tell him if I do find anything out, or if I should be trying to find out anything at all. If I should just leave it alone. It's so difficult!"

"It was very sensible of Bob to clear the air like that. As usual you're making a fuss about nothing," she replied. I can always trust Rosemary to bring me down to earth with her usual common sense. "And there's no way you'll leave it alone! No, he says he wants your help — and you do seem to have done jolly well so far. He wouldn't have said it if he hadn't meant it. But it is his job and he's better placed than you are to make judgments — you can't base a case on *feelings,* however strong they are."

"No, you're right, as usual. I have been — not trying to take charge exactly, but, well, pushing my opinions too much. Oh dear, I hope I haven't been patronizing!"

"You mean because his father used to be your gardener? No, I don't believe that."

"Well, he's always sort of deferential, which, of course, is basic good manners. But I would hate him to think. . . . The fact is, I'll always think of him as a little boy. And actually, it's not just Bob. Michael has a college friend, Will Hornby, who's a very eminent barrister, going to be a judge any day now. But even if he were sitting up there on the bench in his red gown and a judge's wig, I know I'd still see that scruffy young man with the knee out of his jeans, wolfing down my apple cake and asking for seconds, and I'd think *he* couldn't pass judgment on anyone!"

"I know. I find myself asking Roger if he's *really* sure he's left enough time to catch his plane when he's off on one of his important trips abroad, and he's about to become an assistant chief constable! But, as you say, I still see him as that shy awkward boy Jilly brought home from university one summer, who didn't know how to play Monopoly."

I laughed. "Goodness, yes, I remember, and it only seems like yesterday. I suppose," I went on, "I've been too full of myself. While I've been poking about I've completely forgotten that Bob has been working away methodically doing all the important things and keeping track of the big picture."

"Hold that good thought," Rosemary said. "Meanwhile, how do you feel about coming out to lunch at that new place in the Avenue — my treat."

"You mean to say," Norma said, "that she's gone away! Without telling *me*! It's not only inconsiderate, it's bad manners."

"She has been under pressure over a lot of things," I said placatingly.

"Like her husband being murdered," Jean said.

"Well, of course, I understand that. But

nevertheless, there are ways of doing things." She turned to me. "You think it will be for some time?"

"It looks like it," I said. "Unless the police make her come back."

"Is she a suspect then?" Jean asked.

"Well, I don't know about suspect. . . ."

"She certainly had a pretty good motive," she said. "Poor little thing, the way he treated her — and that pathetic son of theirs, too. He'll be glad to be rid of his father."

"I don't think this is the time or the place to go into things like that," Norma said. "The fact remains, if she isn't coming back — back here, that is — then I must see about replacing her. I'll have a word with Alison Rider, my friend from Malvern, and see how she's placed. She did say she'd be interested but I don't imagine she will be able to come straightaway — she's still settling in — so we'll all have to do that little bit extra until she does come. I'm sure," she said, with what she intended to be a pleasant smile, "we'll all pull together."

"What does she think we've been doing all this time?" Jean said sourly when Norma had gone off on one of the mysterious and unexplained errands that seemed to necessitate her absence from the shop from time to time. "And I haven't noticed her doing anything extra." She leaned on the counter and said confidentially, "What do you think? Did Wendy do it?"

"I don't really think she'd be capable of harming anyone. She's such a gentle soul, not very bright perhaps, and she's been kept down for so long I can't see her doing anything violent — seriously though, can you?"

"Oh, everyone's got their breaking point. What is it they say? Even a worm will turn if it's trod on."

"I suppose so."

"She wouldn't do it for herself perhaps, but if it was something to do with John. . . ."

"She's certainly devoted to him. I think she's gone to Birmingham to look after him."

"There you are, then. I suppose they might say it was justifiable manslaughter; is that what they call it? I'd give evidence like a shot about how awful he was to her."

An elderly lady, one of Jean's friends, came into the shop wanting to try on a coat in the window. In the confusion of extracting it and dismantling half the display ("Just as well Norma's not here to see it"), the conversation lapsed.

But it left me feeling uneasy. When I got

home I thought about it again. John had been desperate, was going away. Wendy knew that if that happened, Desmond would never let her see him again. I was sure the idea of leaving Desmond herself never occurred to her. She, who never dared to cross him in quite trivial things, would never have been brave enough to take such a bold step. But . . . but if she'd spoken to John and realized that she'd lose him forever, she might have gone back to the shop (Desmond had said he'd be late home and perhaps she couldn't wait) to beg him to change his mind about John. And then, when he angrily dismissed her, tried to browbeat her contemptuously in his usual bullying way, perhaps something did snap and she snatched up the knife, not, perhaps, with any intention of killing him, but almost as reflex action.

It seemed plausible. Up till now I'd been so carried away by the idea of meek little, downtrodden Wendy — just a surface judgment, really — that I hadn't thought it through. And her placid acceptance of Desmond's death was unusual, to say the least of it. It was all very confusing. I felt that, after all, I'd be glad to leave the whole Wendy thing to Bob, who would have a clearer picture, not clouded by irrelevant feelings about stray cats.

"Did you know that Marcus Stanley is standing for the council?" Anthea demanded.

"Council? What council?"

"The local council," she said impatiently. "I would have thought that Norma would have mentioned it — she's very full of it just now; not surprising, I suppose, since obviously *she* was the one who pushed him into it."

"No, she hasn't said anything to me."

"Mind you, I think they've been keeping it quiet up to now. I only found out from George, who got it from Walter Barrett, who's on the council, and *he* said it had been talked about for quite a while and they've only just decided."

"Oh."

"Well, considering the Stanleys have only been here for such a short while, there was a lot of opposition, but Norma's been getting at people, having these cozy little dinner parties — undue influence, if you ask me."

"I imagine that's how most people get on the council," I said.

"There's been this vacancy ever since Robert Berridge died," Anthea went on, ignoring my cynical attitude to local government. "But a lot's been going on behind the scenes."

"There's no reason," I said, "why Marcus shouldn't make a very good councilor — he's an amiable sort of person and very well off, so there'd be no point in trying to bribe him."

"Really, Sheila! It's a serious matter. The town is being taken over by these off-comers. People who've been born and bred here aren't getting a look in!"

"At least they're willing to *do* things — it would be hard to run Brunswick Lodge without them. You must admit they have their uses."

"They always want to change things. Norma Stanley's forever making suggestions at committee meetings — well, you've heard her!"

"Yes, I know she's maddening. But it does us good to be shaken up sometimes."

Anthea gave a sort of refined snort and returned to her previous grievance. "I'm surprised she didn't put herself up for the council, but I suppose she's got too many other things. And now, of course, she's running that charity shop of yours. She was determined to get her hands on it, and with Desmond Barlow out of the way she's moved straight in."

"I don't think even Norma would resort to murder for the sake of running a charity shop," I said.

"Don't be ridiculous, Sheila. You know perfectly well what I mean. But it's just an example of what I was saying. Soon they'll be running the whole town!"

"I suppose she could have," Rosemary said when I mentioned Anthea's remarks in passing.

"Could have what?"

"Murdered Desmond Barlow."

"I suppose it's possible," I said. "Like I said, she left early that afternoon because she said she had a migraine, but we thought she was just in a huff because of being absolutely furious with Desmond."

"What about?"

"Goodness, I can't remember; there were so many things. Let me think. Oh, I know — Desmond was giving us one of his lectures about how badly the shop was doing, the general implication being that it was all Norma's fault. She was absolutely boiling mad but didn't say anything. Then, when he'd finished, she rushed off home. We thought it was rage rather than migraine, but I suppose one could have given her the other."

"Well, then, she could have come back after you'd all gone."

"But she wouldn't have known there'd be all these other people coming after hours. It would have been quite late."

"She might have been waiting for Marcus to go out or something. Unless he knew what she was going to do."

"*That's* not very likely. Come on, Rosemary. It's all impossible; and, really, wanting to run the shop is hardly a motive!"

"There might have been something in her past. After all, although we know about Marcus we don't know anything about *her* life before they came here."

"No. Positively no. I refuse to think of Norma with a knife in her hand — think of the health and safety implications! Meanwhile, let's be grateful it's Marcus on the council and not Norma — think what havoc she could wreak there!"

After Rosemary had gone I nerved myself to tackle a job I'd been putting off for ages — clearing out the cupboard where I keep some of my pots and pans. I resolutely shut both animals outside (since they are convinced that any activity in the kitchen requires their input), fetched a low stool (I can no longer kneel and crouching down is not an option either) and set to work. It's amazing what extraordinary things one accumulates over the years, oddly shaped tins for baking goodness knows what, baking trays bent to one side from years of use, metal sieves and graters with sharp edges, enormous cast-iron Le Creuset roasting pans almost impossible to lift and a vast preserving pan that would make enough jam to feed a regiment.

I pulled them out of the cupboard and spread them across the floor. Apart from one or two cake tins and the Le Creuset pans (which, since they were too expensive to throw away, I intended to bestow on Thea, who is a good, strong girl), I decided to dispose of the rest. This meant going outside to the woodshed, where I keep the big cardboard boxes, which, of course, meant unintentionally letting in Tris and Foss, who had been keeping vigil outside the back door. I got the boxes and went back into the kitchen just as the phone began to ring. Picking my way carefully among the hardware and the animals, I answered it.

"Mrs. Malory." It was Bob Morris. "I do

hope I'm not ringing at an inconvenient time?"

"Not at all," I said, removing Foss from the arm of the sofa and sitting down.

"I thought you'd like to know — we've got the knife."

"Really! How?"

"A couple walking their dog on West Hill. They'd left the road and were going along one of the paths that lead down to the combe — right off the beaten track. They saw the dog scratching away by a large gorse bush so they went over to have a look. They didn't see anything at first and called the dog off, but it wouldn't come. Then they noticed something, right in the middle of the bush. Fortunately the man was wearing a heavy jacket and gloves so he was able, with the help of his walking stick, to pull it out. It was a knife wrapped up in some sort of material, and the material was stained with blood. So they brought it in to us."

"Good heavens!"

"So I was wondering if you'd mind coming in to the station and seeing if you recognize it."

"Of course. When?"

"I have to go out now, but tomorrow morning about ten — will that be all right?"

"Of course."

It seemed as if things were moving at last. I went back into the kitchen, removed Foss from one of the cardboard boxes, and began to pack away the utensils to put out for the dustman.

CHAPTER FOURTEEN

It was a largish kitchen knife that Bob showed me.

"It looks like it," I said doubtfully. "I mean, it's the same shape and everything. But I can't swear to its being *the* one — there was nothing distinctive about the one in the storeroom."

"How about this, then?" He opened another plastic container and showed me a piece of cloth. It was badly torn, and brown stains covered part of the design.

"Can you open it out for me? That's better. I think — yes, I'm sure. It's one of our T-shirts — or part of it."

"Are you sure?"

"Oh yes, it's the pheasant one. I noticed it specially. Jean and I were joking that Norma would probably throw it out because of it being politically incorrect — blood sports, you know." I shuddered. "Not the happiest of phrases. Sorry."

"And did she? Throw it out?"

"I don't know. It wouldn't be actually thrown out. It was rather a good cotton so it would just go with the stuff to be recycled."

"And where was that kept?"

"There's a box under one of the tables in the storeroom. Then, when it's full, it goes out to one of the sheds at the back until the recyclers come and collect it."

"I see." He thought for a moment. "Desmond Barlow died instantly and he fell just beside one of the tables. I suppose the murderer bent down to remove the knife. I've never quite worked out why — it must have been an unpleasant thing to do and, as you say, there was nothing distinctive about it. Anyway, he (or she) just grabbed what came to hand to wrap it up and wipe the blood off it. . . ."

"And took it away."

"Yes. Why do that? That's another question I can't answer."

"Perhaps they panicked and snatched it up without thinking."

"Possibly . . ." He was silent for a moment; then he closed up the containers. "Presumably, if you're right about the T-shirt, Mrs. Lucas will be able to identify it, too."

"I'm pretty sure she will — it was an unusual design. Will it help to know where it came from?"

"Not particularly, but it all begins to fit in."

"Why on earth would the murderer take it up to West Hill and hide it in a gorse bush? Why not just throw it into the sea?"

"It's not as easy as you'd think. No good doing it at high tide because it might just stick in the sand and be revealed when the tide goes out. And — well — you know how far the tide goes out along this coast. . . ."

"I know. You'd have to walk halfway to Wales just to get to the water's edge and then it would be too shallow."

"No, it was quite reasonable to think that it would be safe in a gorse bush in the middle of the moor. It was amazing luck that particular dog went along that particular path."

"And smelt the blood?"

"Possibly, though it was quite old by then, so it might just as well have been a rabbit it was after. Lucky for us, anyway."

"No fingerprints, I suppose."

"No. Wiped clean, of course. But definitely Desmond Barlow's blood on the fabric."

"So not a lot of help?"

"It always helps to find the weapon. And

if we do manage to find a suspect — well, they would have had to take it up there by car. I mean, you could walk up there from Taviscombe, but not so easily at night, and it would probably have been at night — you know how impossible it is to do anything on even the remotest part of the moor during the day without *somebody* seeing you."

"Perhaps someone saw a car parked along there that night?"

"It's worth making inquiries. We might make a public appeal — that might shake the murderer, to know that we've found the knife."

"Did that inspector ask you about the knife?" Jean asked me.

"Yes. And the piece of cloth."

"It was that T-shirt, wasn't it, the one with the pheasants?"

"I'm pretty sure it was."

"It's weird, really," she said. "When it happened, when we came back here after everything was cleared up, it didn't really sink in. I mean, I knew Desmond was dead, but it didn't seem real. Do you know what I mean?" I nodded. "But seeing the knife and that bit of the T-shirt — well, it brought it home all right. That he wasn't just dead, but he'd been murdered."

"I know."

"Here, in this very storeroom. Right here, where we're standing."

"I know. I try not to think about it."

We were silent for a moment, and then Jean said. "How do you think Norma feels? She's never seemed very upset."

"Perhaps, like the rest of us, it hasn't really sunk in."

"Perhaps," she said doubtfully. "But it isn't *really* the same. For one thing, she stays here sometimes when we're closed. I don't think I could do that. Could you?"

I shook my head. "No, I couldn't."

"I can see she didn't like Desmond and must have been glad to be rid of him, but still, here in the storeroom, all by herself at night. . . ."

"I don't think Norma has much in the way of an imagination," I said. "She certainly wouldn't picture it — what happened here — in her mind. She'd just get on with what she was doing."

"I suppose so. Still, I think it's a bit odd."

"I suppose Inspector Morris asked her about the knife, too?"

"Oh yes. I asked him when I went down to the police station. He asked everybody. *She* didn't say anything about it to me. And that's odd, too, if you ask me."

"Where is she today? She hasn't been in all morning."

"Some sort of meeting. She said it was important — something to do with this place, I suppose — but, of course, she didn't tell *me* what it was."

I suddenly remembered that Anthea had called some sort of extra committee meeting at Brunswick Lodge (that I'd managed to get out of) for eleven this morning. I had a shrewd idea that's where Norma was. But I didn't tell Jean.

"Well, we're not very busy," I said. "So it doesn't really matter."

"We're not very likely to be — busy, I mean." Jean nodded to the street outside, where the rain was being driven along by a strong wind.

"That's true. If it's just rain, people shelter in the doorway and sometimes come in to pass the time in the dry. But no one would want to be out in this unless they really had to."

"I'm afraid I have to, at lunchtime," Jean said. "I promised George I'd go up to the golf club to see if he left his other pair of glasses there. I'd like to go up there at about twelve thirty, because Bill, the steward, will be there then and he's the one who's mostly likely to know. So would you mind taking a later lunch — that is, unless Norma comes back before then?"

"No, that's fine. I brought sandwiches anyway because I didn't want to go out in this weather. But as you say, I doubt if there'll be anyone in."

As it happened, I was mistaken. Just after Jean left and I was thinking of my sandwiches, the door opened and a figure, muffled up in a long raincoat and a waterproof hat, came in. It was Agnes Davis. She deposited her dripping umbrella carefully in the large pottery vase we keep for that purpose, took off her hat, shook the rain from it and came over to the counter.

"Miss Davis," I said in surprise. "Isn't it a dreadful day! What can I do for you?"

She looked slightly affronted at being addressed by name by someone she didn't know, but said, "Can you tell me, please, if Mrs. Barlow is away? I have telephoned several times and yesterday I called at the house, but there has been no reply."

"No, she is away."

"I see. Perhaps you could very kindly let me know when she is expected back."

"I'm so sorry but I'm afraid I don't know — no one does."

"I beg your pardon?"

"She just went — we don't know for sure where she is. She did say she was selling the house, so I suppose she may come back for that."

"Selling the house? She can't do that! And what is happening about the contents?"

"Is there something special you want to ask her about?"

"My pamphlets! I need them for the vicar."

"Oh, I see. And were they in the house?"

"I gave them to Mr. Barlow; he promised to take the greatest care of them — they are quite irreplaceable."

"Oh dear. Well, all I can tell you is that the police are trying to get in touch with Mrs. Barlow — I believe they want to speak to her."

"The police? Why do they want to see her?" She looked at me sharply. "Do they think she is responsible for this terrible thing?"

"Oh, I don't think it's anything like that," I said. "I think they too would like to look for some documents that may be in the house."

"Documents? What documents?"

"I really don't know."

"But what am I going to do about my pamphlets?" she insisted.

A sudden thought struck me. "When did you give them to Desmond — Mr. Barlow?"

"It was that evening — the evening of the day he . . ."

"The day he died?"

"Yes."

"Oh well, then, they won't be at the house, will they? He didn't go back there. . . ."

She was silent for a moment. "Then where are they?"

"I suppose they must be around here somewhere."

"Well . . ." She looked at me expectantly.

"You gave them to him in the storeroom — out at the back?"

"As the shop was closed I naturally went round to the back entrance."

"Of course." I hesitated; then I said, "I'll just go and see if there's any sign of them. What do they look like?"

"They are pamphlets," she said with elaborate patience, "mostly relating to aspects of Christian ritual — there is a very important one dealing with transubstantiation."

"Right. I'll see if they're there."

I went through into the back, leaving the door open so that I could hear if anyone else came into the shop, and looked round in a cursory fashion, but I couldn't see them.

"I'm so sorry. I can't seem to find them," I said.

"Well, really, they can't have just disappeared!"

"No, of course not, but, of course, things have been a bit at sixes and sevens ever since — well, you can imagine, what with the police here. . . ."

"You don't think the police have taken them away?"

"I wouldn't think so, unless they thought they might be relevant to the case."

"What do you mean?"

"Well, they're naturally interested in what happened that evening when the shop was shut, who was here and so on."

"I have already spoken to the police about my visit to Mr. Barlow and I cannot imagine how my pamphlets would, in any way, be relevant, as you call it."

"No, of course not. Well, I'll organize a thorough search. I'm sure they'll turn up."

"They are extremely important. I promised them to the vicar last Sunday — I naturally expected that they would have been returned to me by now. I know that Mrs. Barlow is not the most efficient person in the world — I remember how careless she was about the raffle tickets at last year's summer fete — but I did think she would have seen to my property, and she must have known that those pamphlets were my property and should have been restored to me."

"I think she's been under a lot of stress lately," I said soothingly, "and there has been so much to see to."

"I am fully aware of that. And naturally I have waited until a decent interval elapsed before making my request. But to hear that she's suddenly *decamped* like this, without a word!"

"Actually," I said, losing patience, "she wouldn't have known anything about them if you brought them here to the shop and didn't take them round to the house."

She gave me a hard look. "Very well. I will hope you are able to find them. Father Weston was most interested."

"Father Weston?" I said. "I don't think I've heard of him at St. Mary's. Is he new there?"

"I no longer go to St. Mary's. I find the atmosphere at All Saints much more congenial."

She put on her hat and collected her umbrella and left the shop. Almost immediately after she had gone Jean came back.

"Was that Agnes Davis who was just here?" Jean asked curiously.

"It was."

"What did she want? I don't think I've ever seen her actually in the shop — *she* used to come round the back to see her friend Desmond."

"That's what she came about." I told Jean about the pamphlets. "Have you come across them?" I asked.

She shook her head. "Not that I can remember, and I think I'd have remembered something like that. I mean, we do get some odd things in here, but not religious pamphlets!"

"Perhaps Norma may have seen them."

"Perhaps she threw them out — just the sort of thing she would do." She laughed. "If she has I'd like to be there when she tells Agnes what she's done!"

"Oh dear, perhaps I'd better have a proper look — I will do, after I've had my sandwiches."

"Can you be a dear and put the kettle on? I'm dying for a cup of tea."

"They weren't there," I said to Rosemary. "And I had a really thorough search."

"And you think Norma might have thrown them away?"

"Not thrown them away exactly. We usually put things like that — you know, magazines and old paperbacks — out for the wastepaper. Not the council collection, but a special one that comes every month, and they haven't been since Desmond died. The boxes of the stuff are in one of the sheds at the back, and I had a look through them. There's no sign of the pamphlets."

"Odd."

"I know."

"I suppose someone might have taken them."

"The staff, you mean? Well, it wasn't me and it certainly wasn't Jean, and I can't imagine that Dorothy or Margaret would be interested in a pamphlet on transubstantiation."

"Or Norma?"

"No way. Oh well, Father Weston will have to remain unenlightened."

"Edna was right, then, about Agnes leaving St. Mary's now that Desmond's gone and latching on to the hapless young man at All Saints. Well, I suppose she has to have some interest in her life, poor soul. Edna and her chums will be sorry, though."

"Sorry?"

"Yes, one less thing to gossip about." She laughed. "I wonder if the people who left St. Mary's because of Desmond will come back now."

"I wouldn't think so," I said. "They're safely in the bosom of the Methodists by now."

All the time I was occupied with other things — walking Tris, putting antiflea stuff on Foss (no easy task), taking things out of the tumble drier and deciding they didn't need ironing, preparing the vegetables and the fish for supper, letting Foss out, letting Foss in again — I was thinking about the pamphlets and wondering what on earth could have happened to them. But there seemed no explanation. And then I wondered if I ought to tell Bob Morris. It seemed such a trivial thing to bother him with — and yet any unexplained mystery might just have something to do with the murder, the tiniest thing could provide a clue, or something leading to a clue.

The potatoes and mushrooms were done and I was just about to take the fish out of the oven when the phone rang. Resignedly, I switched everything off and hoped it wasn't going to be a long call.

"Mrs. Malory, sorry to ring you so late."

It was Bob Morris. "I've just got back from Bristol and I thought you'd like to know that Sophie Randall is out of danger and is going to be all right."

"Thank goodness for that. Those poor Randalls have had so much worry! Were you able to speak to her?"

"Just briefly. But it's as we thought — she did steal the money from the till."

"Does that mean . . . ?"

"Yes. Desmond was dead when she went into the shop."

CHAPTER FIFTEEN

"So even though she found him dead she went ahead and stole the money from the till?"

"Yes."

"That's horrible."

"I agree. But she was in a bad state — desperate for drugs and the money to buy them."

"But still . . ."

"She'd gone round the back and seen the light was on in the storeroom so she hung about, hoping whoever was in there would go. After a while she got impatient — like I said, she was desperate — so as the door was open a crack, she looked in and, seeing nobody there (as she thought), she went in. She nearly fell over Desmond Barlow's body, and that really shook her. She said she started to run away; then the need for the money sent her into the shop to rob the till. *Then* she ran away."

"And she didn't raise the alarm — he might not have been dead, only injured."

"She'd just stolen some money — she wasn't likely to phone the police, even anonymously. Her sense of self-preservation was too strong for that."

"How did she know that there was money in the till, anyway?"

"Apparently when no one has time to go to the bank, the money's hidden in the shop. And to show passersby that the till is empty (to discourage burglars), they leave it open."

"Oh yes, of course, Norma told me when I first went there. I'd forgotten. And Desmond obviously hadn't had time — what with all those visitors — to empty it."

"So what time was she in there?"

"Not surprisingly she's a bit vague. After she left the shop she went looking for her drug dealer and couldn't find him for a while until she tracked him down in one of the pubs. He'd been watching the football on the TV there and the match was just finishing — he made her wait until the end. That's why she remembered it. I checked, and the match he'd have been watching ended at ten o'clock. So assuming it took her about half an hour to find him, she must have left the shop at around nine thirty."

"Well, then," I said thoughtfully. "The

shop closes at five, so all Desmond's visitors would have had to go round the back. How about times, then? John seems to have gone in about five, just after the shop closed. We don't know when the man in the suit went in or how long he stayed, but it won't have been that long because Miss Paget was able to see Agnes arrive before she went to switch on her program, which was probably one of the soaps at seven."

"Agnes Davis told me she arrived at quarter to seven and left at half past," Bob said. "So there were around two hours when the murder could have been committed — it helps to narrow down the time."

We were both silent for a moment, considering this. Then Bob said, "What would he be doing so late after the shop closed? Why didn't he go home?"

"Oh, he liked to poke around after everyone had gone — mostly to see what we'd been doing wrong so that he could come and lecture us the next day! Or else think up new ways of doing things."

"Very hands on."

"You could say that! Or I suppose he might have been reading the pamphlets Agnes brought him."

"Pamphlets?"

"She said that's why she went to see him,

to give him some pamphlets. Actually, there's a bit of a mystery about them."

"Oh?"

"Yes. Agnes came into the shop today to ask for them back. I had a good look round but I couldn't find them, and Desmond was killed before he could have taken them home."

"Perhaps someone threw them out."

'I don't think so — I did investigate that. I don't suppose they're important, but I thought I ought to tell you."

"Yes, well, thank you — I'll bear it in mind."

A few days later I was passing the end of Wendy's road and, on an impulse, I thought I'd go and see if she was back. Bob Morris hadn't said anything, but it seemed a good opportunity to take a look, perhaps to see if there was a FOR SALE board outside or anything like that. There was no board, but Wendy's car was parked in the drive.

For a long time after I'd rung the bell nobody answered, but then the door was opened by Wendy, wearing an apron and looking harassed. However, she greeted me cordially and invited me in. The sitting room was cluttered up with boxes and felt cold and dismal.

"Sorry about the mess," Wendy said as she bent to switch on the electric fire. "But, as you see, I'm trying to pack up a few things for the move."

"Did you bring Tiger back with you?"

"No, he didn't like traveling — cried all the way, poor little soul, so I've left him with John."

"Has John got a place at the art school?"

"Yes. I think I told you about one of the people there who were ever so impressed with his work a while ago — well, he's arranged for John to start in the New Year."

"That sounds excellent."

"Yes, isn't it! He's got to do some sort of project — that's what they call it, don't they? I don't understand these things, but I'm sure he'll be all right. He's so happy there!"

"So *you* are definitely leaving then?"

"Oh yes. We're renting a small house for now, but I've seen a really nice little place in Moseley that should suit us very well, as soon as we can sell this place."

There was a pause. Then I said, "Did Inspector Morris manage to contact you?"

"Oh yes, he did telephone. I can't think why he needed to see us again. I'm sure we've both told him everything we can."

"I think there was something about some

of Desmond's business papers he wants to look at."

"It seems a bit silly going on about those. Desmond's been retired for years now — I can't imagine what use any of that stuff would be to him."

"I think he has to explore every avenue, as they say."

"I suppose so, but it seems a great waste of time. But here I am, going on, and I haven't even offered you a cup of tea."

"That would be lovely, if it won't hold you up."

"Goodness me, no — it's lovely to have someone to talk to, and I could certainly do with a cup myself by now!"

She went off into the kitchen and I wandered around the room, looking into the boxes. Mostly china and ornaments. But one box, on the table, had papers in it. Lying on the top were some pamphlets. Cautiously, listening for Wendy's return, I took one out. It was torn, as if someone had tried to tear it in two, but the title page was still perfectly readable: "Transubstantiation: What It Means for Us Today."

I put it back in the box on top of several others. It was obvious they were the pamphlets Agnes had asked about. But how had they got back here? There seemed to be only one answer, and I simply didn't know what to do about it. My first instinct was to tackle Wendy about it straightaway. But really, I thought, it should be done by Bob Morris; it was, after all, his job. But then, by the time I'd got in touch with him, she might have got rid of them — it seemed as if she'd tried to destroy at least one. I heard Wendy coming back and quickly moved away and sat down on the sofa.

"Sorry to be so long. Funny, isn't it, the way the kettle always takes ages when you're in a hurry."

She was carrying a large tray with the tea things on it, and I got up and went over to the table.

"Here," I said. "Let me clear a space for you."

As she put the tray down I felt it was too good a chance to miss, so I casually leaned over and picked the top pamphlet out of the box.

"This looks interesting."

She looked up from pouring the tea. "Oh, that's just some of Desmond's old stuff," she said quickly. "I was going to throw it away." She put the cup of tea on one of the little tables beside me and offered me a biscuit.

I shook my head. "No, thanks. But, Wendy,

I don't think you should throw any of Desmond's papers away until Inspector Morris has had a chance to look at them."

"Oh, that isn't anything to do with Desmond's business," she said airily. "It's just some of his old church things."

I hesitated for a moment and then I held up the pamphlet and said, "I think this is one of the pamphlets Agnes Davis was asking about the other day. She came into the shop especially to ask about them."

"Oh."

"She was very anxious to have them back because she wants to lend them to someone."

"Oh well, she's welcome to them," Wendy said shortly. "I'm sure I don't want any of that stuff cluttering up the house. Like I said, I was getting rid of all the old rubbish."

There was a pause and then I said, "We were wondering what had happened to it — to them, really; I gather there were several pamphlets. The thing is. . . ." I took a deep breath. "The thing is, Agnes Davis brought these particular pamphlets into the shop for Desmond on the evening that he — well, that he died."

I looked at her inquiringly but she didn't say anything.

"Since Desmond didn't come back home that evening," I went on, "the question is how did they get here?"

The silence seem to last for a very long time. "I brought them back," she said.

"You mean you went back to the shop later on?"

"Well, the time was getting on and I was worried about John, and Desmond had said he was coming home to speak to him and John wasn't here. And Desmond didn't come and I didn't know what he was going to do about it all. After a bit, I couldn't stand waiting any longer, so I put on my coat and got the bus and went to the shop."

"When was this? What time?"

"I don't know. I didn't notice. It was quite late by then because I got the last bus."

"But that would have been after ten!"

"I suppose so."

"But Desmond was dead by then."

Another silence, even longer than the last one.

"I know," she said.

"You mean," I said slowly, "that you went into the shop and saw him there? Dead."

"Yes."

"And you didn't do anything about it?"

"There was nothing I could do. He was dead. I had to get back — I'd no idea where

John was and he might have been trying to ring me."

"You didn't call the police."

"I told you I had to get back for John."

"But . . ."

"Anyway, I didn't want to get mixed up in all that."

I didn't know what to say. There seemed no way of getting through to her the enormity of what she'd done. It was like dealing with an uncooperative child.

"What about the pamphlets, then?" I said at last.

"Oh them." She looked at the pamphlet I still had in my hand. "A lot of old rubbish," she said. "*She* was always using them as an excuse to see him, calling in at the shop at all hours of the night. I know what people were saying — it's not very nice to have people saying that sort of thing about your husband. I wouldn't have minded if she'd been something to look at, but she was nothing but a dried-up old spinster. If they'd been having a proper affair — I could have understood that. But no, it was all this church stuff. Just friends, he said — intellectual stimulus, if you ever heard of such a thing — funny sort of friends, meeting on the sly like that."

"It must have been hard on you."

"So you see," she said eagerly, "why I couldn't leave those things there. What with all the fuss there'd be about his death and everyone talking about it — people would know she'd been there."

"Yes, but . . ."

"I didn't want that."

"The next day," I said, "when they asked you to identify the body, why didn't you say anything then?"

"It was too late. I'd have got into trouble — you know what they're like. Anyway, it wouldn't have made any difference. I wasn't going to stir up trouble all for nothing."

"But Wendy," I said, "you're going to have to tell them now."

"I don't see why. Like I said, it doesn't make any difference."

"Inspector Morris wanted to know what happened to the pamphlets."

"Oh, those stupid things!"

"And," I continued, "he'll want to know how they got here."

"You're not going to tell him?"

"I'm afraid I have to."

"I thought you were my friend. You were so good about Tiger and everything."

"I am your friend, Wendy, and that's why I'm saying that *you* must tell Inspector Morris all about it. He's a nice man. I know he'll understand what a difficult situation you were in."

"I don't know. . . ."

"Would you like me to ring him and ask him to come round here now?"

She considered this for a moment. Then she said, "And you'll stay?"

"Of course. Can I use the phone in the hall?"

As I dialed the number I prayed that Bob would be in the station. Miraculously, he was.

"Bob, I'm so sorry to bother you, but something quite extraordinary has happened. Can you *please* come to Wendy Barlow's house right away? She's here and there's something very important she needs to say to you."

"Well . . ."

"Honestly, you need to see her here."

"Right. I'm on my way."

Bob must have left right away because he arrived quite soon, which was a relief — conversation was not easy and was confined to talk about John and how well he was doing. When the bell rang Wendy looked at me beseechingly and I went to let Bob in. While we were in the hall I told him briefly about the pamphlets and what Wendy had told me about her movements that evening.

"I honestly believe she has no idea that what she did was wrong," I said, and when he went into the sitting room he spoke to her gently, in a quiet, friendly way with simple, easy questions.

"Well, now, Mrs. Barlow," he said at last. "I think the best thing will be for you to come with me back to the station, where we can get all this written down properly."

"Oh, I don't know. . . . I've got so much to do here."

"It won't take long, and we'll send you back home in a police car."

This promise seemed to appeal to her, and she said, "Oh, all right then. I'll just go and get my coat and lock up the back door."

When she had gone out of the room I got up and took the other pamphlets out of the box and gave them, together with the partly torn one, to Bob.

"I'm so sorry to have called you out like this," I said, "but I was so afraid she might have destroyed these and I thought you needed to see them *here* — evidence, I suppose."

"Absolutely. No, I'm most grateful that you were on the spot at the right time!" He smiled. "As you have a knack of being."

After a great deal of fuss about handbags and front door keys, Wendy finally got into

Bob's car and was driven away.

The whole episode was so extraordinary that I felt in the need of some rational conversation. So I rang Rosemary and told her all about it.

"She had simply no idea that what she'd done was wrong," I said. "It's like dealing with a child."

"Well, Desmond always treated her like a child, so I suppose she just became one," Rosemary said. "Anyway, she was never allowed to grow up properly."

"Oh?"

"Her parents died in a car crash when she was about ten and she was brought up by a fierce old grandmother, very strict, always telling her what to do."

"I never knew that."

"Oh, Mother — of course — knew all about it. Church contacts. Apparently the grandmother wouldn't let her mix with other children and young people because the parents left all this money and she had this thing about fortune hunters."

"Poor Wendy. But how did she come to marry Desmond?"

"Oh, the grandmother lived in the Midlands, and Desmond went to the same church. I expect Desmond made up to her to get to Wendy. And, of course, she thought he was such a nice young man, a lay reader and well in with the vicar, so she encouraged it."

"You think he married Wendy for her money?"

"Partly, but partly because he didn't want a wife so much as a doormat and obviously Wendy was very good doormat material. And that's what she became. Never had a thought in her head he hadn't put there. Except about John, though he was as weak and spineless as she was."

"Oh dear. Well, anyway, she couldn't have murdered Desmond, even if she did go back to the shop — he was dead already."

"Are we sure of that?" Rosemary said.

"What do you mean?"

"She could just as well have gone back there earlier, in that gap when he was still alive and before Sophie found him."

"But she said. . . ."

"After all this, can you really trust anything she says?"

Chapter Sixteen

"You were absolutely right," Bob Morris said wearily, when he rang me later. "She didn't seem to realize that finding your husband dead was something you should report to the police!"

"Did you believe her?" I asked. "About the time she went back."

"I don't know *what* to believe. Can she really be as naive as all that?"

"I think she is," I said and I told him about her past life. "I don't believe she'd be capable of anything devious. I mean, she'd have to be a pretty good actress to have kept up that act all these years!"

"I suppose so."

"Actually, you might have a word with her next-door neighbor (the one on the right-hand side). She seems to keep a fairly watchful eye on Wendy — I think she worries about her. She might just have seen her going out that evening — after all, it was most unusual — and have noticed the time."

"Good. I'll do that. Anyway, I'm going there tomorrow to look through any business papers that might have survived. I don't think she's thrown *them* away because she said they'd be in her husband's desk and she seemed nervous about opening it."

"That doesn't surprise me! Well, good luck. Just be grateful she didn't bring her cat back — you'd never get her to talk about anything else if it was there."

When I got to the shop next morning I found Jean alone.

"Where's Norma?" I asked.

"Don't ask me!" Jean said shortly. "She was out of that door before I'd even taken my coat off. Muttered something about a meeting — believe that if you want to!"

"It certainly seems a bit much when there's just the three of us."

"Exactly. We haven't heard anything lately about this friend of hers from Malvern who was going to be such a wonderful asset. We've got a couple of boxes of china that need looking at and half a dozen pictures, all waiting for this so-called expert of hers! Say what you like about Desmond, but he always got things done."

"I have a sort of feeling," I said, "that the

friend from Malvern isn't going to material-
ize — not here, anyway."

"Really?"

"I did hear — Brunswick Lodge gossip,
but it's usually reliable — that she and
Norma had a great falling out. All to do
with the arts committee there. I think this
'friend' was trying to take over, something
like that, anyway."

Jean gave a snort of laughter. "One in the
eye for Madam! She wouldn't dream of letting us know, of course, but it does leave us
in a hole. I think Dorothy might come in
for a few extra days, but it's not satisfactory, and I'm going to tell Norma so when
she gets back."

"I must say, I'm surprised Norma hasn't
been more hands on since she took over. I
thought it would be Desmond all over
again. She's altered the window display and
moved things around a bit, but since that
first burst of energy, nothing much at all.
You know how she used to go on about how
old-fashioned all Desmond's idea were. I
was expecting something really revolution-
ary."

Jean looked thoughtful. "I get the feeling
that there's something wrong there."

"What sort of thing?"

"I can't put my finger on it. But like you

said, she hasn't really taken *over,* has she?"

"Exactly."

"And she's in and out all the time — and doing what? You can't tell me that it's all to do with this place."

"She's on a lot of committees; perhaps she's finding it difficult to fit everything in."

Jean shook her head. "I don't think it's that. It's like — oh, I don't know — as if she's worried about something. I went into the storeroom the other day and she was talking on her mobile, so it wasn't shop business."

"And?"

"She finished her call in a hurry when she saw me come in, but I did hear her say, 'Don't do *anything* until you hear from me.' She said it quite sharply, as if it were important."

"It could be something and nothing."

"It didn't sound like that to me. Oh well, let's have a cup of tea while we can."

I was really quite tired when I got home. The weather had been dull and overcast and the holiday makers, for want of anything better to do, trailed in and out of the shop all day, pulling things out of the racks, taking them off hangers and leaving them all muddled up so that there was a great deal of tidying up to do at the end of the day. Norma was out all morning and a lot of the afternoon, only appearing just in time to collect the takings for the bank. Jean spoke to her quite sharply about our being left alone to cope. Normally this would have provoked an even sharper reply, but Norma just nodded absently, muttered something about "seeing to it" and went off into the storeroom. It did seem that Norma was not, to put it mildly, her usual self.

The animals were being difficult, too. Although Tris cleared his dish and looked up hopefully for more, Foss was in one of his fussy moods and rejected the food from a newly opened tin, making offensive scraping movements with his paw to show his distaste. I opened a different tin and, although he ate a single mouthful, he turned away and uttered a loud Siamese cry of complaint. Eventually I did what he knew I would do. I took some cooked chicken from the freezer and warmed it up for him. He gave me a look of triumph and ate his way steadily through it, scattering particles of food all over the floor. I gave Tris extra biscuits as a reward for being cooperative and poured myself a gin and tonic as a reward for getting through a tiresome day.

I was just wondering what I could bear to

cook for supper when the phone rang.

"I hope this isn't a difficult time for you?" It was Bob Morris. "But I thought you'd like to know what I found today."

"From Desmond's papers?"

"That's right. I had a bit of a job getting Mrs. Barlow to open the desk. First of all she said she didn't know where the key was, and then that her husband wouldn't like it!"

"She probably expected Desmond to rise from his grave and forbid it!"

"Something like that. Anyway, when I insisted, she 'remembered' where the key was. She opened the desk and more or less bolted from the room."

"Goodness! So, did you find anything useful?"

"Oh yes, everything was in labeled files, mostly church stuff, but there was a file for George Arnold. Not a lot in there — I got the impression neither of them wanted to put very much down on paper."

"But enough to be helpful?"

"Apparently they worked together on a development in the Midlands, and recently some sort of problem seems to have arisen and there's going to be an inquiry. From the very guarded references in their correspondence, I gather that Arnold had given

Barlow some false information — told him something was OK when it wasn't — to get the project under way, and now he wanted Barlow to back him up in a lie."

"And Desmond, pillar of the church, wouldn't."

"Something like that."

"That sounds like a pretty good motive."

"It could be. I'll have to go and see him — try and get some idea of his movements."

"Miss Paget said he left before Agnes arrived. That would be before seven. She said he didn't stay long; presumably Desmond wouldn't agree to anything. But, of course, he might have gone away to think about it and decided to give it another try."

"Certainly. Anyway, I must have a word with him. It would certainly make things simpler if he really has got a strong motive — anything to do with money is so much easier to handle than all this emotional stuff!"

"I can see that a jury would find Wendy pretty difficult to understand."

"Fortunately I don't think it will come to that," Bob said. "I took your advice and had a word with her neighbor. She *had* seen Mrs. Barlow go out that evening. At about a quarter to ten. As you said, she thought it was most unusual."

"So she would have taken the ten o'clock bus and Desmond would have been dead long before she got to the shop."

"That's true. One thing bothers me, though. Why would she have taken the bus, and presumably have had to walk all the way home — the neighbor didn't see her come back — when she could have driven in by car?"

"Oh, that's easy. She's never driven after dark. She told me that Desmond would never allow her to, so now she's too nervous to attempt it."

I could almost hear him groan. "Well," he said, "I suppose it's a good thing to have all that business with Mrs. Barlow out of the way. Mind you," he went on, "I'm far from satisfied with her son's story. I might stop off in Birmingham and have a word with *him* when I'm chasing up this Arnold man. Though that can't be until next week — I've got a stack of paperwork that should have been done last month and I daren't leave it any longer!"

After all that it seemed simpler to have a poached egg on toast rather than attempt anything more complicated. I'd just settled down with my tray and an undemanding television program when the telephone rang. I tried to ignore it, but, of course, you never can.

"Sheila, I'm sorry to bother you, but I had to speak to someone!" It was Wendy Barlow, sounding very agitated.

"What is it? What's happened?"

"It's that police inspector — he's been round here. He made me open Desmond's desk!"

"Yes?"

"And he took away some papers!"

"I'm sure he gave you a receipt for them," I said.

"Well, yes, he did, but that's not the point. Desmond would have been so angry. He never used to let me even *dust* that desk."

"Desmond isn't here anymore," I said, rather more briskly than I would have done if my egg hadn't been congealing and my toast getting soggy.

"Well, of course, I know that. But even so, is he allowed to *take* things like that?"

"If they're relevant to the case."

"But how could they be?"

"I don't know, but I'm sure Inspector Morris will return them to you when he's finished with them."

She was silent for a moment. Then she said, "He asked me for John's address in Birmingham. Why do you think he did that?

You don't think he believes *John* knows anything about the business. Desmond would never tell John anything. . . ." Her voice trailed away.

"I expect he has to ask everyone — just routine."

The word seemed to satisfy her. "Well, if you think so. He wanted to give me back those stupid pamphlets, but I said I wasn't going to take them and he should give them back to *her.*" I spared a moment's sympathy for Bob Morris. "Anyway, I've got enough to do packing up things here."

"Have you had any luck with selling the house?"

"Someone made an offer. It wasn't the full price but I told the agent to take it — I just want to get away."

"And the police are all right with your going?"

"Why wouldn't they be? I haven't done anything wrong. I need to go to Birmingham as soon as I can. I'm sure John isn't getting proper meals, and he has to leave Tiger alone all day, poor little thing."

She seemed inclined to go on at length about these two subjects, but the mention of meals made me cut her short with vague good wishes for the future. I threw away my ruined supper and settled for a cup of hot chocolate and a piece of Victoria sponge.

"Apologies for absence," Denis Painton said at the beginning of the Brunswick house committee meeting the next day. "Mrs. Stanley."

"She wasn't here at our last meeting either," Anthea said.

"That's not at all like her. She's always so keen, such an asset," Muriel Mabey said. She's one of Norma's few fans on the committee.

Anthea ignored her. "What's going on?" She turned to me. "You work with her, Sheila. Do you know what's the matter?"

"I really don't know," I said. "She's been in and out of the shop a lot lately. I expect she's just busy."

"Well, it's not good enough. We're all busy, and if people can't be bothered to turn up for meetings they shouldn't be on the committee at all."

"She's only missed two meetings," Denis said mildly. "There may be some problem at home."

"I don't see poor old Marcus causing any problems," Jennifer Richards said. She, too, has had several run-ins with Norma. "No, I expect she's taken up with all this business of getting the poor chap onto the council —

241

hasn't got time for Brunswick Lodge now!"

"I still say it's wrong that off-comers like him should be on the council at all," Anthea said, returning to a well-worn theme. "Both of them pushing their way into everything like this. And, anyway, if you *do* take on these responsibilities, then the least you can do is take them seriously, not just turning up when it suits you."

"I don't see why Marcus Stanley shouldn't do perfectly well on the council," Alan Berwick said.

"He's got some sound ideas about the new car park. I was having a chat with him the other day. . . ."

"At one of Norma's little dinner parties, I suppose," Anthea said.

"Well, yes, as a matter of fact it was," Alan replied stiffly. "But I don't see what that's got to do with it."

"I think we might get on with the meeting," Denis raised his voice a little. "Has anyone any ideas on who we might get to conduct the sixty/forty auction next month and who will be responsible for organizing the collection of the items donated."

I didn't have the time or the inclination for the next few days to bother much about Norma and the shop and the Brunswick

242

house committee because Tris tore his leg quite badly on some wire when we were out and I was back and forth with him to the vet. He's an old dog, and there was a worry with him about the anesthetic, but he came through quite well, just a bit dopey for a while. The main problem was trying to make him keep on the sort of lampshade affair he had to wear round his neck to stop him chewing the dressing.

"He keeps walking backwards," I told Rosemary when she rang to inquire for the invalid. "As if he could somehow back out of it, poor little thing."

"I know, Alpha was the same when he had that accident. There's nothing you can do about it. In the end I just gave up, took the wretched thing off and left him to it!"

"But what about the dressing?"

"He worried at it a bit but I gave him one of those enormous chews and he concentrated on that."

"I hate the way they staple the wound together — it seems all wrong! Still, I'll give it a bit longer, but I expect I'll take it off. Foss isn't helping — he refuses to go anywhere near Tris because of the disinfectant smell from the vet, and obviously he resents all the fuss the poor old boy is getting."

In the end I did decide to take off the

cone-shaped collar, and I'd just got Tris settled with chews that I hoped might distract him from his dressing when the phone rang. I picked up the receiver while trying to keep an eye on Tris and answered it rather irritably.

"I'm so sorry — is this a bad time?" Bob Morris said. "You sound a bit distracted. Only I did want to give you a piece of news before I have to go out."

"No, it's fine," I said, recovering myself. "What news?"

"It's about George Arnold. Among all the paperwork that had piled up was something from the traffic division. Apparently, he was picked up by a patrol car for driving while using his mobile phone."

"Good heavens!"

"It was a few miles outside Bridgwater and it was timed at seven twenty."

"And Desmond was still alive then, talking to Agnes." I thought for a moment. "I suppose he might just have turned round and gone back to Taviscombe."

"Unlikely. He seems to have gone on and joined the M5 on his way back to Birmingham."

"So you won't have to go and see him."

"No, but I shall send that correspondence to the West Midlands police. It might help the inquiry."

"Oh well, there's one perfectly good suspect gone," I said. "What about John Barlow, then?"

"Yes, I must talk to him. He hasn't got any sort of alibi and I can't rely on *anything* his mother says. . . ."

Tris seemed perfectly happy with his chews and did no more than sniff at the dressing the whole evening. Foss, on the other hand, prowled restlessly around the house, complaining bitterly about the unequal division of treats until pacified by a slice of the cold roast lamb I was keeping for supper.

Chapter Seventeen

"Glad you could come to lunch," Rosemary said. "We've been given a whole side of smoked salmon, and Jack and I will never get through it on our own. Anyway, I hardly ever see you now you're at that shop, not to mention all the time you're helping the police with their inquiries. Is everything all right with Bob Morris?"

"Oh, we're fine, now we've sort of cleared the air." I took another sandwich. "This smoked salmon is really special. Anyway, how about you? You're looking a bit under the weather."

"I'm worried about Mother. Mrs. Wilson has just died."

"Oh yes. I saw that in the paper last week. She was a good age."

"That's the trouble, really. There aren't many of Mother's old friends left. Only a couple, and they're house-bound or in a home; there's nobody left to come to tea anymore, no one to chat to about old times. She feels lonely — you know she was never one to make friends with a younger generation — so she's got very depressed."

"Oh dear."

"I go in every day, and Jilly and the children are very good, but they've all got such busy lives. Still, it's a bit of a strain. Of course, we're so lucky she's got Elsie, though she's well into her seventies now."

Elsie, usually referred to by Mrs. Dudley as her housekeeper, is much more than that — cook, cleaner, full-time caregiver and, really, a good friend.

"Goodness, yes. She's a marvel."

"Mother doesn't seem to take an interest in anything. I got her CDs of some of the Dick Francis novels because she can't read for very long now, but she's hardly played them. Says she can't manage the machine, which is nonsense — she managed it perfectly well before Mrs. Wilson died."

"Would it help if I went round?" I said. "I want to ask her about Edith Seaton — she was Marcus Stanley's aunt, you know, the one who brought him up."

"Splendid! That should perk her up. Can you manage Monday? That's always a gloomy day for her."

■ ■ ■ ■

When I arrived at Mrs. Dudley's, Elsie whispered to me in the hall, "She'll be so glad to see you, Mrs. Malory. She's been very down lately. I know you'll cheer her up."

Certainly, when I went into the sitting room I was shocked to see how much frailer she looked.

Knowing how critical she always was about my choice of flowers, I'd been in despair until I found some freesias. As I proffered them to her, she gave me one of her rare smiles and said, "Thank you, Sheila dear. I'm very fond of freesias; I had some in my wedding bouquet." She touched the petals gently with the tips of her fingers and handed them to Elsie with precise instructions as to which vase she should put them in.

"Well, Sheila, it's good of you to come and see me when I know how busy you are with that shop of yours."

"Actually it has been busy this last week or so," I said. "Poor Wendy Barlow hasn't been in, of course, and Norma — you know Norma Stanley; she's the new manager — hasn't spent much time in the shop either."

"Ah yes, poor Mrs. Barlow. I hear she's moving away — Birmingham, isn't it? It seems an odd sort of place to go to."

"Her son is at the art school there."

"I was surprised she felt able to make such a big move; I seem to remember she was quite a helpless little thing."

"Not now," I said, and I noticed that, from being slumped in her chair as she was when I arrived, she was now sitting upright.

"Really?" Her voice was much stronger.

So I told her all about Wendy's amazing transformation, and by the time Elsie came in with the coffee and cake and the freesias in their special vase, she was quite animated.

"And you say she didn't murder that husband of hers? Well, I'm not surprised *someone* did. Such an unpleasant man. I remember one of the antiquarians' expeditions — quite local, Brakeley Court. He held forth at great length about the house and the family. I stood it for as long as I could — you know how I hate making a fuss — but eventually I had to correct his inaccurate rubbish. When he had the impertinence to contradict me, I pointed out that I had lived here all my life and was personally acquainted with the family and he, as a newcomer, was unlikely to be better informed than I was."

"Good for you!"

Mrs. Dudley bowed her head in acknowl-
edgment. "I didn't have any more trouble
with *him,* then or on any subsequent occasion. If that wretched little wife of his had
stood up to him — but there, some people
are born helpless."

"A bit like Marcus Stanley," I said.

"Marcus! What nonsense. He was chris-
tened Mark — a good Christian name. I
suppose it was that wife of his who made
him change it. And why? may I ask."

"I expect she thought Marcus sounded
more distinguished."

"All of a piece with her silly pretentious-
ness. And now I hear she's managed to get
him on the council."

"I believe she gave dinner parties for all
the influential people — or people she
thought were influential."

"I heard about that. Alan Berwick and
Robert Mabey — influential! Heaven help
Taviscombe if *they're* influential."

"It seems to have worked," I said.

"Oh well, I suppose he can't make the
council any more inefficient and useless
than it's always been."

"Well, at least he has some connection
with Taviscombe. He told me he used to
spend his school holidays with his aunt,

250

Miss Seaton. What was she like?"

"A *difficult* woman."

"Difficult" usually meant simply someone who disagreed with Mrs. Dudley, but the force with which she said the word indicated something out of the ordinary.

"It's no wonder," she went on, "he's grown up to be such a poor creature, brought up by that woman."

"He did say she was a bit austere."

"Well, I suppose that's one way of putting it. As you know, Sheila, I have my standards; I belong to a generation that knows right from wrong and I have very firm views on how people should behave." She paused for my nod of approval. "But Edith Seaton still lived in the Victorian age. No idea how to bring up a child — of course, she never married, even though she was quite wealthy."

"I gather she was fond of bridge."

"Fond — she was obsessed by it! She used to have afternoon bridge parties — the only time she ever saw people — and really, you'd think every game was a matter of life and death. So stupid. All card games are a waste of time when you could be doing something useful."

"Did you play bridge?"

"Well, I *could,* of course, just enough for

social purposes. Everyone did. I went to one of these parties once, but really, I couldn't bring myself to go again; such a dreadful atmosphere."

"I imagine she'd have been quite unpleasant if people didn't take it as seriously as she did."

"She had a very sharp tongue. A lot of people never went again."

"I'm not surprised."

"Of course, there are always a few who are prepared to put up with unpleasantness where there's money. Vera Parker was one of her hangers-on. Vera used to tell me about that poor child, how strict she was with him, never allowed to make friends with local children — so sad."

"Marcus — I mean, Mark — said she left him the house and the money because he was her only surviving relative, but he did say she was quite fond of him."

Mrs. Dudley smiled pityingly. "Well, I suppose you would be fond, in a kind of way, of someone you've dominated completely."

"I suppose that's why he married Norma. I mean, perhaps he needed someone who'd boss him around."

"*She* knew when she was on to a good thing. His parents had made a lot of money abroad but they were killed in an air crash or something and he inherited everything. That's when she married him. He set up a business of his own somewhere in the Midlands, Kidderminster or Redditch — some peculiar-sounding name like that. Vera couldn't remember. Well, when I say he set it up, she was the driving force."

"I can imagine." I took another slice of ginger cake. "I believe she didn't get on very well with Miss Seaton. Mark didn't say anything directly — I suppose that would have implied criticism of Norma and he adores her — but that was the impression I got."

"She would have disapproved of anyone Mark married. I suppose if he'd chosen some little mousey creature she would have accepted it and bullied her, too. But to be faced with someone as strong-minded as herself — well!"

"Oh dear!"

"And it's not as though the girl *was* anybody. Edith Seaton was a terrible snob. She would have swallowed her feelings if there had been good connections, but there was nobody — no family and no money. Apparently she'd just been some sort of typist who'd managed to get her claws into him. So after the first couple of times they weren't invited down there again."

"But she still left him the house and money," I said. "She could have left it to a charity — is there a Home for Indigent Bridge Players?"

"He was the only surviving relative — she had very strong opinions about the importance of the family. She may have disapproved of Norma Stanley, but it would have taken something really terrible for her to have disinherited him."

"I bet she'd be turning in her grave if she knew how Norma has modernized the house, *and* she's planning a swimming pool!"

"That doesn't surprise me in the least — just what I would have expected of that sort of person." She looked at me inquiringly. "She must be very difficult to work with in that shop of yours."

"She's not easy," I said with feeling. "Though, strangely enough she's been distracted lately. There seems to be something on her mind, and she's hardly been in the shop at all."

"Well!" Mrs. Dudley said triumphantly. "That confirms it."

"Confirms what?"

Mrs. Dudley leaned forward. "Vera Parker, when she telephoned me a while ago, said there was some problem about money."

"Really? But Mark is very well off."

"It's all about investments, so Vera said. Well, not Vera exactly — she's in West Lodge now and she's become very friendly with this man there, Harold Porter. He's been in there ever since his wife died; men are so helpless. Apparently he used to be something to do with finance and he knew the Stanleys."

"Oh yes, I remember him, a nice man. He and his wife used to come to Brunswick Lodge —"

"Yes, yes," Mrs. Dudley interrupted me. "He told Vera that when the Stanleys first came to Taviscombe, Mark had just sold his business in wherever it was and was looking round for suitable investments. They had some sort of stockbroker in London, but after a while *she* decided that she was a financial genius and more or less took over. Well, you can imagine! Vera and I have been waiting for the crash to come."

"And you think that whatever is on her mind is something to do with these investments."

"Well, of course," she said impatiently. "What else would it be? I must telephone Vera this afternoon after she's had her rest. Harold Porter will be very interested, too."

I saw, with pleasure, that she was seeing a

whole new vista of gossip and speculation opening up before her.

After I left I went down to the seafront to get a breath of fresh air. The terns, back from their summer banishment, were lined up on the rails, waiting hopefully for human largesse, while the larger gulls circled overhead, making louder demands. It was a calm, overcast day. The sea and sky merged into a sort of pearly gray blur while the sea itself hardly seemed to move.

As I was standing there, thinking with satisfaction of Mrs. Dudley's new animation, a car drew up beside me and Bob Morris got out.

"I thought it was you," he said. "I was going to ring you."

"Has something happened?"

"I finally managed to get up to Birmingham to see John Barlow."

"I hope he was more forthcoming than his mother!"

"A bit, but he was a mass of nerves, so frightened that anything he might say would convict himself or his mother."

"Not surprising he's nervous, I suppose, if you think of both his parents!"

"I did finally manage to get out of him that, in desperation, he'd confronted his father when he went to the shop. He didn't tell his mother what he was going to do, just said he was going out."

"That must have been what I heard when I gave her a lift home that afternoon. I was sure I heard voices when she was in the kitchen making the tea. Obviously that didn't go well."

"No. His father's comments were particularly brutal, I gather, and when he'd finished, the boy said he just rushed back home, threw a few things into a bag and got a bus into Taunton to catch the Birmingham train."

"Wendy told me he'd gone back to university," I said. "I suppose she had some muddled idea that university seemed more normal, and, of course, she didn't say anything then about the row with his father. So when I spoke to him on his mobile, he was actually in Birmingham, not Nottingham."

"That's right. Apparently the only person he felt he could turn to was this person who'd been sympathetic and tried to get him into the college of art."

"So his father was still alive when he left him. Or do you think he was lying and that he went back later and killed him?"

"Well, he did have a strong motive and he

didn't have an alibi — I mean, his mother's word wouldn't really be enough."

"True."

"He said he caught the six thirty bus to Taunton to get the Birmingham train."

"Difficult to prove."

"Almost impossible." He paused. "*But* I was lucky. On the off chance I asked the woman in the refreshment room if she'd been on duty that evening and she had. And she *did* remember him."

"No!"

"It seems he ordered a coffee, and just as he was about to drink it, the Birmingham train came in and he chucked it down on that ledge over the counter and rushed to get on the train. Of course, the coffee went everywhere — all over the cake and sandwich display. A terrible mess to clear up. You can imagine how something like that would have stuck in her memory!"

"How amazing. And she was sure it was him?"

"I'd got a photo of him from Mrs. Barlow — you can imagine how difficult that was — and she identified him from that. But she said she'd noticed him specially when he came in because he was so agitated."

"What a tremendous piece of luck! So John *has* got an alibi."

"Absolutely."

"And that's the last of your real suspects," I said almost reluctantly. "Nobody else with a real motive?"

"Not that we know of. Oh well, I must be getting along. I'm collecting Dad and taking him back to supper with us — it makes a bit of a break for him."

"That's nice. I've been meaning to drop in on him — I found a DVD of that Victorian kitchen garden program and I thought he might enjoy it."

"Sounds like just the job, as he would say. Thanks very much."

Rosemary rang me next day, sounding much more cheerful.

"Thanks, Sheila — a real transformation!" she said. "She's hot on the trail of Norma Stanley now. In fact, she asked me to drive her to West Lodge to have tea with Vera Parker and this friend of hers. She likes going to West Lodge — it means she can feel superior to all the inmates there because she's still living at home."

"I thought she seemed more herself when I left. Fancy her going out!"

"I know. It's been ages. She made me go all through her wardrobe with her, item by item, before she decided what she was going to wear."

"That is a good sign. And it will feel like old times for Vera Parker again, so everyone's a winner."

"Do you really think there's something wrong with the Stanleys' finances?"

"I don't know, but it would explain why Norma has been so offhand about the shop — something I never imagined would have happened."

"Oh well, I expect Mother will get to the bottom of it," Rosemary said confidently. "She usually does."

The noise of a crash from the kitchen and a sharp yelp from Tris made me ring off hurriedly. Needless to say, it was Foss, who in his investigation of the dishes on the work top, had knocked off a bowl of stock (mercifully cold), which had splashed Tris and shattered into many pieces. Tris was whimpering and demanding comfort, and I suspected that Foss had taken refuge from my wrath under the duvet in the spare room. The Herculean task of clearing up this mess drove all thoughts of Norma Stanley right out of my mind, at least for the moment.

CHAPTER EIGHTEEN

The next couple of days when I was in the shop, Norma hardly went out at all. Instead she spent a lot of time in the storeroom — rearranging the stock, she said — and sorting through the stuff put aside for the dealers. But quite often when I went through she was just standing, some garment or object in her hand, apparently lost in thought.

"I wish to goodness she *would* go out," Jean said to me. "It gives me the creeps to see her mooning about in there. It doesn't look as though she's actually *doing* anything — and that's not Norma! Anyway, having her there makes me feel awkward about going through to the kitchen to make the tea. Not that she seems to notice."

Anthea, too, when I saw her at Brunswick Lodge, was also puzzled.

"Whatever's happened to Norma?" she demanded. "She's hardly come to any committee meetings and she sent a message — didn't tell me herself — that she couldn't organize the transport for the sixty/forty sale. After all the fuss she made about doing it! *And* she phoned Julia to say that she wouldn't be able to write to the man about that string quartet after all. Well, Julia was furious that she hadn't even gone to the arts committee meeting to explain. It's left her in a very difficult position." Anthea couldn't keep a note of satisfaction out of her voice since she and Julia (to put it mildly) don't get on.

"I don't know," I said. "She's not been herself at the shop. Perhaps she's got something on her mind."

"That's all very well," Anthea said. "But if you take on these things you ought to see them through. I suppose she's too busy pushing poor Marcus on the council — telling him what to say at council meetings, I daresay."

"Perhaps," I said. But I was wondering what Mrs. Dudley had found out. It must have been something really serious to account for Norma's unusual preoccupation.

I was quite busy the next few days. Thea had a bad cold so I collected Alice from school (Norma didn't even make a sarcastic remark when I left the shop early) and gave her her tea. Afterwards, when she'd done her homework, we watched my ballet DVDs while Alice gave me a running commentary, enthusiastic if inaccurate, on the performers, frequently prefaced by "Hannah says. . . ." Hannah being the fount of all ballet wisdom since she had actually seen *Swan Lake* at Covent Garden.

"So could we go, Gran? At Christmas. It could be my Christmas present. I wouldn't want *anything* else!"

I made the usual noncommittal reply ("That would be lovely — we'll see what Mummy says") and suggested that she might give Tris a run around the garden before she went home.

When I went to have a new battery put in my watch I saw Marcus in deep conversation with the jeweler over what looked to be a very expensive diamond-and-ruby ring. The jeweler seemed to be examining it closely and commenting on it. Marcus hadn't seen me, so I said I'd call back later to collect my watch and went out of the shop quickly. It occurred to me that Marcus might be selling some of Norma's jewelry and I didn't want to embarrass him.

"Goodness," Rosemary said when I told

her. "Things must be in a bad way. Norma's got what Mother calls some very nice pieces — I suppose they'd fetch a bob or two."

"I've more or less given up wearing rings," I said, fingering my wedding and engagement rings, "except for these. I looked at my hands one day and saw how veined and wrinkled they were and it seemed like an insult to decorate them in any way! I've put them on one side for Thea and Alice."

"I know. And don't you find necklaces feel so *heavy* nowadays? Pearls are all right, but that ornate gold-and-lapis one that Aunt May left me just gives me a headache. I don't suppose Delia would want it — too old-fashioned — or Jilly, for that matter. Still, I suppose they could always sell it."

"Like poor Marcus."

"Poor Marcus," she echoed. "Bad enough when there was plenty of money — Norma would be all right with the 'for richer' bit, but not so good with the 'for poorer.' Especially if it was her bad judgment that caused it, though I bet she'd be the last one to admit that."

"I'm sure Marcus would never even suggest it," I said. "He obviously adores her, no matter what. He's obviously completely under her thumb."

"Talking about being under the thumb, Mother has set me an impossible task. She says she wants a small table for the sitting room."

"But there are hundreds of small tables in that sitting room — you can't move without running into one!"

"Ah, but there isn't the *right* small table."

"Oh."

"The one she wants has to be of a certain height, a certain size and of the right color wood. Oh yes, also of the right period and the right price."

"Oh dear."

"Exactly."

"So what are you going to do?"

"Go and see what they've got at the auction rooms. And you are coming with me. Please."

"You want someone to blame if it's wrong?"

"Yes. So will you?"

Taviscombe is unusual for a town of its size in having rather a good auction room. I suppose it serves a wide catchment area where there are still some quite large houses with expensive pieces that might be up for sale. I thought Rosemary might actually find a table there that fulfilled all Mrs. Dudley's requirements, except, perhaps, the reasonable price.

There were only a few people there when we arrived, looking over the items ready for the next sale, so we were able to have a good look round.

"Just look at that splendid chiffonier!" I said. "Who on earth would have room for a massive thing like that? And that enormous wardrobe — I bet you could wander into Narnia though the back of that."

"I can't see any small tables," Rosemary said, "except this one, which looks far too expensive." She indicated a delicate Regency table with small gilded sphinxes for feet.

"I don't think that's quite what your mother has in mind, anyway. There must be a sale catalog somewhere. Let's go and see if we can find one — I expect Rory is somewhere about."

Rory Bartlett is the auctioneer, a jolly man who kindly gives his services to Brunswick Lodge when we have a fund-raising auction there. He is also very knowledgeable and a sharp businessman.

We found him peering into a large brass-bound trunk.

"Hello, Sheila, Rosemary. Amazing what the military carted about all over Europe in Victorian times."

"It's very handsome," I said, "and very evocative. I always make a beeline for Wellington's traveling medicine chest whenever I visit Apsley House." I looked at the brass letters let into the lid of the trunk. " 'J.S.C.' Anyone famous, do you think?"

"We haven't any sort of documentation, unfortunately — that would up the price."

"Just another officer taking the necessities of life to India or the Crimea," I said. "I wish we knew."

"We were wondering," Rosemary said briskly, "if there's a catalog of the sale that we could have a look at?"

"Were you looking for something special?"

"A small table for my mother."

"Ah." Rory had had many a brush with Mrs. Dudley over the years. "In that case you will need to take your time and consider most carefully." He winked at me. "I'll just go and get you one from the office."

He came back with the catalog and seated us on two Victorian chairs at a handsome Pembroke table in front of an enormous, heavily carved bookcase. "Here you are, then. I hope you find something in there."

We leafed through the catalog in mounting despair. Everything was either unsuitable or too expensive. We were preparing to give up when we heard Rory in conversation with someone on the other side of the bookcase.

"Yes, I see," he was saying. "It's a very fine piece — rather large, of course; that might be against it. But it's a superb example and we would be delighted to handle it for you. Although you might feel you could get a better price at one of the London auction houses?"

"No, we would rather deal with you." It was Marcus's voice. Rosemary and I exchanged glances.

"That's splendid," Rory went on. "Our catalog goes online, of course, and that means we get a fair number of overseas buyers making bids. I do believe a piece like this would have great appeal to the right collector."

"That's fine, then." We could hear the relief in Marcus's voice. "I'll just check with my wife."

"Excellent." Rory was obviously delighted to get such a desirable piece. "When we hear from you we'll go ahead with the arrangements. If you'd just like to come into the office, I'll take the details." Their voices died away.

"Well!" Rosemary said. "First the jewelry, now the furniture. What next? Shall we pop round the corner and see what it is they're selling?"

"Better wait a bit until we're sure Marcus has gone. We don't want him to see us looking at it."

It was a beautiful lacquer cabinet, exquisitely inlaid. "Eighteenth century, do you think?" Rosemary asked.

"I don't know. I remember seeing one like that in a museum dated back to Charles II."

"Norma must be absolutely desperate if they have to sell something like this. Think how she must have enjoyed showing it off."

We moved away reluctantly and returned to the catalog for one last look.

"It's no good — there's nothing here. I'll have to see if there's anything at the auction place at Crewkerne, but it's a long way to go. . . ."

Rory came back. "Did you find anything suitable?"

Rosemary shook her head. "Most of it's out of our league."

Rory smiled. "I think there's something over here that might just suit." He led the way to a sort of annex. "These things aren't in the sale, but I thought this might be what you're looking for."

He pointed to a small (but not too small) Late Victorian table in mahogany with a piecrust edge and cabriole legs.

It was charming. We both nodded vigorously.

"It's lovely," Rosemary said. "But it looks expensive. What do you think it will fetch?"

He named a sum that was surprisingly low. "It's reproduction," he said, "but very good reproduction. And the vendor's going abroad and wants to get rid of it quickly so it needn't go into a sale. I think it's a bargain."

"It certainly is!" Rosemary said warmly. "Can I write you a check now? I think even Mother will be pleased with that."

"I think she will," Rory agreed, "as long as you don't tell her that *I* recommended it!"

Norma continued to behave oddly at the shop. She was out quite a bit again.

"A relief, really," Jean said. "We're better off without her, the way she is now. But it's getting beyond a joke being so short staffed. I don't know what's been done about getting someone to replace Wendy — we may have to put a notice in the window asking for volunteers."

"Norma wouldn't like that," I said.

"Well, she'd have to lump it," Jean replied shortly. "We can't go on like this."

"We're managing."

"Not really — lunchtimes especially, with just the two of us. I have to go out and get a proper lunch because Ted and I have our main meal at midday, but you don't. It isn't fair your having to bring sandwiches all the time and never having a proper break."

"I don't mind."

"It's the principle of the thing. If Norma's too busy to run this place," she said, echoing Anthea, "she ought to give it up and let someone else do it."

"Do you fancy doing it?" I asked.

"No fear. Too much like hard work — *when* it's done properly. No, I just like the company really, and a bit of a laugh. Not that it's been a lot of laughs lately. Not, of course," she added, catching herself up, "the way things are — poor Desmond and so forth."

"It has rather changed things," I said.

"How about you?" Jean asked. "Would you like to do it?"

"Goodness, no. Anyway, I'm only temporary, filling in until Monica comes back."

"That's a pity; we'll miss you. When *is* she coming back?"

"I don't know. She hasn't been in touch lately."

I had to admit to myself, though, that I'd be reluctant to leave until the mystery of

Desmond's death had been cleared up. But I hardly felt able to say so to Jean. Instead I offered to go and make the coffee.

On my way to the kitchen I saw that Norma had left a file on one of the tables in the storeroom. Something sticking out caught my eye. It was a letter on very expensive paper and I was just able to see the heading, which was that of a national firm of house agents — the sort of grand ones who advertise in *Country Life*. The temptation to open the file and have a look was very strong, but just then Jean came through, saying, "There's a lady in the shop who wants a copy of *Lorna Doone*. I'm sure I saw one the other day in that box out the back. Could you just have a look?"

I found the book. When the customer had gone, Jean said, "You see how awkward it is, just the two of us. I shouldn't have had to leave someone alone in the shop like that. As it was, she was all right, but if it'd been someone a bit doubtful I'd have to have said we hadn't got it and lost the sale. That's the sort of thing I mean!"

I agreed with Jean absently, my mind on what I'd seen. Then Norma came back and Jean ostentatiously went out to make the coffee, remarking as she went that it was possible to do so now that there were *three* people in the shop.

"First the jewelry, then the furniture, and now the house!" I said to Rosemary. "Things must be pretty bad. Any news from your mother's informants?"

"Nothing yet. Mother's getting very impatient — she says Harold Porter is a broken reed."

"I don't see how he's going to find out anyway," I said. "Client confidentiality, and all that."

"I know, but apparently Vera says there are Ways."

"Well," I said grudgingly, "I suppose if your mother's on the track. . . ."

"She approved of the table, by the way. She did a complete volte-face; said how marvelous Rory is and how clever it was of him to find it."

"One thing I will say about your mother: she's never been inhibited by consistency!"

"What about Norma, though. Do you think they're staying in Taviscombe or moving right away?"

"Oh, moving away surely," I said with conviction. "She could never bear to live here in a smaller house with a diminished lifestyle. I'm sure she'll find some very *grand* reason for leaving. It's poor Marcus I feel sorry for, having to leave the family home, even if he didn't have a very happy time there. It was the one stable thing about his childhood."

"Still, he won't have Norma pushing him on the council. That's if she stays with him now he's poor."

"Not that poor with the money from the house and everything."

"Perhaps there are *debts* as well," Rosemary said. "If they lose everything and are really poor, then we'll see if she sticks by him."

"Except that we'd never know because they'll have been long gone."

When I went into the shop next morning, I found Margaret there as well as Jean.

"Margaret's very kindly giving us an extra day," Jean said.

"That's nice," I said.

"Because," Jean went on bitterly, "Madam is not here and won't be here for the next two days."

"Really?"

"She telephoned me last night, *at home,* to say she had to be out of town for a few days and would I look after things!"

"I suppose it might be urgent family business," Margaret suggested tentatively.

"I wouldn't know," Jean said. "She put the phone down before I could ask anything."

The next day was a Saturday, when I normally didn't go in, but I didn't feel I could let them down. When, at the end of the day, Jean said, "If she isn't here on Monday I'm going to close the shop — I don't care what anyone says," I felt she really had a point.

I was clearing out the fluff from the tumble drier and pondering, as I always do, the strange fact that the fluff caught in the filter is always gray, no matter what color the garment was that shed it, when the phone rang. It was Rosemary.

"The most extraordinary thing," she said. "Mother went to tea with Vera and Harold yesterday and he says that there's no question of the Stanleys' investments failing. On the contrary — and this annoyed Harold very much — they're better than they've ever been. It seems Norma's a financial wizard!"

"No!"

"As I said, Harold's very put out, having prophesied dire disaster. Mother's not too pleased either."

"But . . . but if they're not in financial dif-

ficulties, why all this — what do they call it?
— all this downsizing?"

"Exactly."

"Well," I said, "it's beyond me — I can
only suggest you get your mother onto it
right away!"

CHAPTER NINETEEN

"What's really interesting," Rosemary said, "is if they haven't lost all their money, then why are they selling up?"

"I hadn't thought of that."

"You'd think Norma would want to branch out, especially now she's got Marcus onto the council. Lots more dinner parties, much grander plans for the house — she could be the queen of Taviscombe with all that lovely money."

We worried away at the problem for a while but reluctantly decided to await events.

"And that," Rosemary said, "is admitting defeat."

"I promise not to tell your mother."

Strangely enough, the next day Norma came into the shop wearing what looked like the diamond-and-ruby ring I'd seen Marcus apparently selling in the jewelers'. I made a point of admiring it, though normally I refrained from doing anything that would increase her self-esteem.

She smiled complacently and said, "It is rather lovely, isn't it? Marcus bought it for me — it was our wedding anniversary yesterday."

I murmured something that might be taken for congratulations.

"He's very good about things like that," she went on. "Anniversaries, birthdays, special occasions."

I was surprised; I don't think I'd ever remembered her praising him before.

"Still," I said to Rosemary when I reported back, "it *was* a particularly handsome ring. I suppose even she might be grateful for that."

Norma continued to be absent from the shop, without any explanation, and didn't even reprimand Jean for putting a notice about volunteers in the window.

"I can't understand it," Jean said. "Not a word — well, she even said it was a good idea. Honestly, it seems to me that she's completely lost interest in this place."

"Not just here," I said. "She's almost completely given up going to Brunswick Lodge, and with all the committees she's on and the things she's supposed to be organizing — well, you can imagine the chaos. *And* bad feeling!"

"What do you think she's up to?"

"I've no idea, and really, I don't think I'm brave enough to ask her."

"Well," Jean said resolutely, "if no one else will, I shall; we can't go on like this. Anyway," she continued briskly, "while she's out I'm going to have a go at some of those boxes in the storeroom."

When I went through later she was examining the contents of a large cardboard box.

"Have you any idea of where these came from?"

"Good heavens," I said, holding up one of the books. "I do believe this is a first edition." I took some more books out of the box. "Yes, this one, too, I'm almost sure, though I need to look it up."

"What are they then?" Jean asked.

"A whole collection of Rudyard Kipling. Terrific."

"Kipling? The one who wrote that poem?"

"That's right."

"Oh. And you think they're valuable?"

"Some of them look quite rare."

"I didn't think anyone read this sort of stuff these days — too old-fashioned." Jean picked one of the volumes out of the box and looked at it suspiciously. "I mean they haven't been made into telly plays or any-thing."

"He's having quite a revival," I said. "So no doubt there may very well be a TV play before long."

"Oh."

"I wonder who they belonged to." I examined a couple more of the books. "Oh yes, there's a bookplate in this one. Let me see — oh, Alfred Lyle. He died a little while ago, didn't he?"

"Back in March, I think it was," Jean said. "I remember seeing it in the *Gazette*. He used to be a headmaster; there was quite a lot about him. I expect his wife's having a bit of a clear-out."

"I remember her," I said. "I met her a couple of times at Brunswick Lodge. They were friends of Denis Painton; he brought them to some of the concerts." I looked through the books again. "I wonder if she realizes how valuable these might be? I mean, if she doesn't then we ought to tell her — she might want to sell them."

"I don't know," Jean said doubtfully. "They were given to us. Desmond would have kept them, no questions asked, and I expect Norma would do the same."

"Yes, but I really think. . . ." I put the books back into the box and pushed it out of sight under the table. "I'm going to ask her; it's only fair. For all we know she might need the money. I don't know how well off they were."

"Can you think," I asked Rosemary, "of any reason why the Stanleys should be selling the house?"

"Perhaps they're moving into something grander?"

"The present one's pretty grand, especially if Norma puts in that swimming pool and landscapes everywhere. No," I said, "I'm beginning to wonder if they're planning to leave Taviscombe altogether."

"Why on earth would they do that?"

"I don't know. But all this business of Norma losing interest in the shop and not bothering about all the stuff at Brunswick Lodge — it would make sense."

"But surely Marcus wouldn't want to sell his aunt's house; it means so much to him."

"Oh, come on! When has anything that Marcus wants mattered to Norma?"

"Where would they go?"

"London, I suppose."

"Oh no," Rosemary said decidedly. "Norma knows that her best bet is to be a big fish in a small pond. In London she'd be nobody."

"True. But where then?"

"Goodness knows. I'll just have to have a word with Mother and see what Harold can turn up."

"Sheila, you see Norma at that shop of yours. Do you have any idea what she's playing at?" Anthea button-holed me in the kitchen at Brunswick Lodge when I was washing up after the Monday coffee morning.

"What do you mean?" I asked innocently.

"You know very well what I mean. She's missed nearly every committee meeting in the last few weeks."

"She sent apologies for her absence. Pressure of work, she said."

"*What* work? Has she taken over the shop now that Desmond's gone? Is that it?"

"She is in charge now," I said hesitantly.

"But?"

"Well, actually she hasn't been coming in much lately."

"You must admit it's very odd. Not like her at all. If she can't be bothered to turn up for things, there are plenty of other people who'd be only too glad to. I told Denis we should have a meeting about it and make our feelings known to her."

"What did Denis say?"

"Oh, you know what he's like, never takes the initiative in anything."

"Perhaps it's just a temporary thing," I suggested.

"Oh, it's not just Norma. Alan says that Marcus hasn't been at some of the council meetings." She looked at me suspiciously. "What do you make of that?"

I emptied the washing-up bowl and hung the dishcloth over it. "I haven't the faintest idea," I said. "We'll just have to wait and see."

"You're as bad as Denis," Anthea said irritably and went out of the kitchen, closing the door behind her with unnecessary violence.

"Guess what," Rosemary rang me in some excitement. "Harold says that Norma is liquidating some of her assets."

"What does that mean?"

"I think she's selling some of her shares and things."

"People do — they invest in something else."

"Yes, but Harold says it's very odd that she's selling things at the wrong time."

"The wrong time?"

"Something to do with the state of the market, Harold did explain. Anyway, he thought it was most peculiar."

"Perhaps they *are* going; they might need extra money for that. Anthea was saying that Marcus hadn't been to some of the council meetings — it's all of a piece. But why all the mystery?"

"I know. Usually Norma can't wait to tell everyone what wonderful project she's embarked on. Unless . . . unless it's something bad, disgraceful even. She wouldn't tell anyone then."

"What on earth could that be? Perhaps Marcus has had enough and has left her," I suggested, "and she's getting out with everything she can lay her hands on."

"Not likely. Anyway, he can't have gone — I saw him in the bank yesterday."

"In the bank? I suppose you didn't see what he was doing there?" I asked hopefully.

"Um, no, not really. There were a couple of people in front of me so I couldn't see. Whatever it was, the girl on the counter was away for quite a long time. Sorry."

"Oh well, it was too much to hope for. Still."

"Absolutely."

I did ring Alfred Lyle's wife about the Kipling first editions but there was no reply, so I pushed the box of books farther out of sight to prevent Norma finding them, put the whole thing out of my mind and concentrated on other things. Norma's absences were becoming even more frequent. When Jean challenged her about them she replied evasively, even placatingly.

"I'm *so* sorry," she said. "I do know how awkward it must be for you and I do appreciate it. It won't be for very long, I promise you."

"So what do you make of *that*?" Jean demanded. "Norma being conciliating — I couldn't believe my ears. I was so flabbergasted I couldn't ask her what she meant before she was off again."

" 'Not for very long,' " I said thoughtfully. "I wonder. . . ."

"Wonder what? You mean she might be giving up the shop?"

"Yes . . ." I broke off. Somehow I didn't feel I wanted to share my theory about the Stanleys leaving Taviscombe with Jean. She would probably challenge Norma about it, and I didn't want her alerted to the fact that anyone knew what she was planning.

"Yes," I repeated. "It would certainly explain things."

"But why would she do that?" Jean demanded. "After the way she's worked to get things her own way here — all that arguing with Desmond. It doesn't make sense."

"Perhaps now Marcus is on the council she wants to concentrate on that."

"I suppose it might be that," she said reluctantly. "But where does that leave us?"

"They'll probably make you manager," I suggested. "After all, you know more about the shop than anyone."

"Oh, I don't want the responsibility. No, they'll bring someone in from outside and heaven alone knows what sort of person we'll get."

"Well, whoever it is," I said, "they couldn't be worse than Desmond and Norma."

"There's definitely something up," I told Rosemary. "The question is what."

"And why. What on earth would make Norma want to up sticks just when everything is working out so well for her? It doesn't make sense."

"Unless something we don't know about has gone wrong. Maybe she's done something wrong and is going to be found out."

"Such as what, for goodness sake?"

We were both silent for a minute. Then I exclaimed: "Desmond — perhaps *she* murdered him!"

Rosemary looked at me inquiringly. "But

I thought she had an alibi."

"Only from Marcus. But," I added reluctantly, "there's no sort of motive, except dislike."

"It would make sense, though — I mean, make sense of why she's behaving like this."

"Well, yes. But why now?"

"Perhaps your inspector chum has uncovered some new evidence."

"I suppose. . . ."

"There's no reason why he would have told you, especially if it's something he's still working on."

"True. And I can't very well ask him."

We were both silent again, considering the possibilities.

"So what *exactly* happened that day? I mean about Norma."

"Let me see. Oh yes, Desmond gave us one of his lectures about how badly the shop was doing and how it was all our fault. As you can imagine, Norma took it all very badly."

"I can imagine."

"As soon as he'd gone she flounced off home."

"Flounced?"

"Well, you know what I mean. She was absolutely furious — just snatched up her coat and stormed off." I stopped suddenly.

"I've suddenly remembered something. She took her coat, she grabbed it from the peg where we hang them on her way out. But — *but* I'm pretty sure she didn't take her handbag."

"So?"

"I don't know if her handbag was there the next morning when they discovered Desmond's body, but if it was there I'm pretty sure Bob would have asked us all whose it was, and he never mentioned a handbag. I'll check with him."

"And Norma hadn't tried to go in to work that morning?"

"No, she was still having her migraine. At least that's what Bob said when he tried to contact her about the till."

"Aha! And none of you thought she had a migraine when she went off."

"Goodness no — it was just that she was livid with Desmond."

"So," Rosemary went on, "she could have come back later that evening and killed Desmond and seen her handbag and taken it away then?"

"Hang on, let me think. I'm sure there was a gap when someone could have killed him before that poor girl came in and saw him when she robbed the till. Between seven and nine, I think it was."

"Too much to hope that someone saw her."

"Bother Miss Paget and her TV! Still people do use that back alley as a shortcut. It's not impossible. I think I'd better have a word with Bob."

But when I asked for him at the police station, they said he was away on a course.

"What do they *do* on all these courses?" Rosemary said crossly when I told her. "Snatching him away like this when he's in the middle of a case. Oh well, I'll have to get on to Harold again and see what he's turned up."

Alas, Harold had no more news for us. "A broken reed, Mother says," Rosemary reported. "So I don't know where we go from here."

Norma continued to come and go at the shop at erratic times, and Anthea said that even Denis was contemplating action at Brunswick Lodge.

"He's calling an extraordinary committee meeting," she said with some satisfaction, "to ask her what her intentions are. And if she doesn't deign to come to that, we'll vote her off in her absence."

"Can you do that?" I asked. "I mean, does the constitution allow it?"

Anthea is a great one for the constitution.
"We'll do it, even if we have to make an amendment!" she said grimly.

It had been a particularly tiresome day at the shop. There were very few customers, and we always found standing about boring. We could have done useful things in the storeroom, but it was a hot, sticky day and, with no real ventilation, it was like an oven in there, so we just hung about, drinking tea and longing to go home. To make things worse, Norma hadn't come back to go to the bank and we had to "hide" the takings. Jean was particularly vociferous about this.

"After what happened when Desmond died," she said, "you'd think she'd make a point of being here. I mean, if only she'd told me she *wasn't* coming back I could have gone myself. Now it's too late. It isn't," she continued bitterly, "as if I haven't had to do it umpteen times before when she's gone swanning off." She thumped her empty tea mug down on the counter. "Anyway, it doesn't feel safe having all that money in here."

"It's not an enormous amount," I ventured. "Today hasn't been a very good one — it never is when it's sunny. Everyone's on the beach or the seafront."

"That's as may be. It's the principle of the thing. Well," she said resentfully, "if something happens and the place is robbed again, don't let anyone blame me!"

When I eventually got home I was feeling fractious, too; the car was hot and the road was closed and I had to go miles out of my way to get home. The house, too, was hot and airless and the animals, who also hate the heat, were particularly difficult, picking at their food or, in Foss's case, refusing it contemptuously and demanding "the other food." I left the back door open so that they could go in and out without persecuting me, and went to change into something cooler. Because I was irritable, I wrenched my pearl necklace off and broke it. Fortunately, there were knots between the pearls so they didn't scatter, but knowing I'd somehow have to make time to take it in to be mended made me crosser than ever. So when Tris came into the sitting room bearing a large crust that I'd put out for the birds and began chewing it messily on the carpet, I spoke to him sharply. He flattened his ears and looked at me anxiously and, of course, I felt dreadful.

"Oh, poor Tris, I'm *so* sorry — I shouldn't take my bad temper out on you!"

While I was getting him some treats to assuage my guilt, Foss came in (attracted, as always, by the thought of Tris having something he didn't) and so he had to have some, too, and by the time I'd done that and made my supper (half a grapefruit and a poached egg on toast), I was more or less recovered. But I was still wondering where Norma had gone off to *this* time, and what on earth was going on.

In the sitting room, with the windows open and a gin and tonic to aid concentration, I tried to think of a satisfactory motive — any motive — that might have led Norma to kill Desmond. As far as I knew they'd had no sort of contact outside the shop and it seemed most unlikely they'd known each other before the Stanleys came to Taviscombe. The only thing I could think of was that somehow Desmond had found out something discreditable about Norma; after all, we knew very little about her past. But even if that was so, it would be difficult to find out what it was. Unless, perhaps, there was something illegal about her finances — our only hope there was Harold, and although he'd been very helpful ("How on earth did he find out all these financial things?" I said to Rosemary. "I wouldn't dream of asking," she replied.), there was obviously a limit to what even he could do.

The next day I took my necklace in to be mended. To my surprise I found Marcus there again. This time he saw me come in, and, just for a moment, he looked slightly embarrassed though he greeted me with a smile and a half wave of the hand before turning back to the jeweler. Fortunately the assistant was busy with another customer and, by pretending to look at a showcase full of watches, I was able to have a good look at what Marcus, who had his back to me, was doing. He seemed to be interested in a diamond pendant. I heard the jeweler say, "As you can imagine, we don't have much demand for pieces of that quality — you'd need to go to London for something like that, Hatton Garden perhaps. I could give you the address of a reputable dealer there, if that would help?"

Unfortunately the assistant was now free so, reluctantly, I had to leave this fascinating conversation and get on with my own business.

Needless to say I phoned Rosemary right away.

"Why would he be buying Norma more jewelry?" she demanded. "She's already had her birthday!"

"It didn't sound like ordinary present buying," I said. "More sort of commercial — I mean, Hatton Garden diamond dealers?"

"Oh, I don't know — Eva Makepeace kept going on about that diamond bracelet her husband bought her for their ruby wedding. He bought that somewhere in Hatton Garden."

"Yes, but . . . it didn't *sound* like that. Not personal."

We were both silent for a minute. Then Rosemary exclaimed triumphantly: "Of course — realizing their assets!"

"What do you mean?"

"What if they're moving abroad and want to put their money into something portable, you know, like the Russian aristocracy did in the Revolution."

"But why go to all that trouble? Why not just transfer their money somewhere abroad?"

"Perhaps they couldn't do that, perhaps they're running away — from whatever it is that's making them move — and don't want to be traced?"

"But surely they'd have a job getting them out of the country; what about customs?"

"Oh, I'm sure there are ways," Rosemary said airily. "People are always doing it in books and films."

"How?"

"*I* don't know. They could hire a helicopter, or Norma could go back and forth wearing a few bits at a time — lots of ways."

"I suppose you may be right," I said doubtfully. "Still, it does sort of make it likely that they're planning to move abroad. Oh dear, I do wish I could speak to Bob about all this. He'd have ways of finding out."

"I don't think we're doing too badly," Rosemary said cheerfully. "You must just keep your eyes and ears open when she's in the shop — listen to her phone calls."

"I'll do what I can, but I don't think she's likely to do anything incriminating there when she could be doing it at home!"

But as it happened Norma did take a call when I was in the shop kitchen. The storeroom door was half open and she didn't know I was there.

"And you have confirmed the flights to Zurich for the thirtieth? Excellent. And the car hire? Very good. I will be in touch next week to confirm the final arrangements. Good-bye."

At that moment Jean called her into the shop to deal with the person who valued the porcelain for us and who had a problem.

So while Norma was tied up with that, I was able to leave the kitchen and the storeroom without her being any the wiser.

"Switzerland!" Rosemary was delighted. "Swiss banks and all that — they really must be going."

"But on the thirtieth," I said. "That's less than a month away. And they're hiring a car; they could be going anywhere."

"Not necessarily."

"And I'm sure it's difficult to actually go and *live* in Switzerland."

"Lots of celebrities do."

"I expect that's different."

"So come on. If they're going soon, we haven't got much time."

"To do what?"

"Well . . . Talk to your friend Bob when he gets back. He ought to know they're leaving."

"I don't know if they *can* while the case is still going on."

"Wendy went to Birmingham."

"But she has an alibi. And you must admit, even Bob must see it all looks very suspicious."

"Perhaps."

"Anyway, I'm sure Norma will have thought of some very good reason — business or whatever — for them leaving. After all, Marcus's firm was something to do with abroad. She could make it look as though it had all been arranged ages ago. *We* know that she's only just started to liquidize her assets."

"I don't think Harold would be willing to explain to the police how he knew that."

"Oh, I'm sure the police can find out that sort of thing," Rosemary said airily.

"That's all very well. But even if they could, I don't think it would be proof."

"We need to find something, and fast."

"Yes," I said, "but what?"

We were both silent for a moment. Suddenly it all seemed very difficult.

"I suppose," Rosemary said slowly, "they must have made arrangements for their furniture and stuff to be moved. I know — I'll ask Andy Seymour."

Andy Seymour ran the only large removal firm in Taviscombe.

"He'll think it a bit odd — your asking, I mean."

"Oh, I'll think of something."

"And does his firm do shipping abroad? They might have got someone from Taunton, or even Bristol. We'd never find out if they have."

"Well, it's worth a shot."

■ ■ ■ ■

Alas, Andy Seymour proved to be another broken reed.

"So it must be a Taunton firm," Rosemary said. "We must try and keep an eye on the house."

"I don't see how that would help," I said crossly.

"We might be able to find out where they'd gone."

"Yes, possibly. But they might leave before the move. If it's as urgent as all that, they might have to get out as soon as possible. Anyway, if they were still there and anyone saw the removal van, surely someone would ask awkward questions."

"We've got to do something before the thirtieth; we haven't got much time."

"Well, Bob should be back long before then."

But when I phoned the police station they said that he'd gone on leave.

"That really is tiresome!" Rosemary said. "Where do you think he's gone?"

"*I* don't know. But even if I did, what use would that be?"

"Well, you're on good terms with him. You could just give him a quick phone call."

It seemed a bit of a long shot, but when I was passing the end of the road where Bob's father lived, on an impulse I went along to the house and rang the bell. Old Mr. Morris was very welcoming.

"Come in, come in. It's good to see you."

He led the way into the conservatory and, after I'd admired his fine display of pelargoniums, we sat down and he said, "It's good to have a bit of company. Bob and Molly are away."

"Really?"

"Yes, it's very sad. Molly's mother, Amy, lives in Sidmouth. She moved down there after Alfred died. You remember him — he used to work at Woods in the furniture department. Well, she went to live with her sister, Maureen, but *she* died two years ago, so Amy's been on her own."

"I'm so sorry."

"She liked it down there and she made a lot of friends. You know how well she always got on with folk. But one of her friends rang Molly and said she really didn't think Amy should be on her own. She was getting very forgetful, kept leaving the back door open, things like that, and once she left the gas on and nearly had a fire in the kitchen. Getting very vague, too, not remembering what day it was. Like I said, things like that."

"Oh dear."

"So they thought they'd better go down and see what was happening."

"Of course."

"It wasn't easy for Bob to get away; he's still busy with that case — you know the one we were talking about. But they were very good about it. Bob said they were waiting for more evidence or something like that; I don't understand these things. Molly's sister Josie had the children, so they didn't have to be taken out of school. Anyway, when they got down there they found things were worse than they'd imagined.

"Poor Molly."

"Well, the way things were, they decided she really had to go into — what do they call it now? — sheltered accommodation, an old people's home."

"That's very sad."

"I mean, Molly would have had her back up here, but with the children and Bob away sometimes it wouldn't have been easy."

"No, it wouldn't."

"So they're down there looking at places. Molly said there was a very nice one, and one of Amy's neighbors was already in there, and when they took her to see it she seemed to like it."

"That's good."

"But, of course, there's so much to arrange."

"I expect they'll have to be down there for quite a while."

"Well, Bob will have to come back soon, but if she does go into this place there'll be the house to see to. Although Molly says she can manage, he's going to stay as long as he can."

"Well, he would need to. Poor souls, it must be very difficult for them."

"So it seems," I said to Rosemary, "that he's going to be away for a bit. And really, I don't think I can phone him when everything's so difficult there."

"I suppose not," Rosemary said regretfully.

Things hadn't improved at the shop; Norma was hardly ever there. Jean's irritation was mounting, and her threats to phone headquarters were more frequent.

"I just hope she hasn't forgotten I'm away for a week next month," she said. "She'll have to arrange for Dorothy to come in every day. You can't manage on your own."

"I expect she's made a note of it," I said soothingly.

"She might not have done."

"Oh?"

"I phoned her when I first knew we were going to see my sister Freda in Bournemouth. I wanted to do it straight-away so no one else would get that week first, and I didn't want to ask Desmond because he was always so awkward about things like that. So I phoned her at home that day when she rushed off and said she had a migraine. Of course, I didn't believe for a moment she had one — you remember what a temper she was in! Anyway, when I phoned she really did sound awful, so I felt quite bad for bothering her. I wondered why she answered the phone herself if she was in such a state, but she said she thought it was Marcus — he'd gone out to get something for her."

"That was the night that Desmond was killed."

"That's right. So you see, what with all *that* commotion, she might have forgotten."

"What time did you phone her?"

"What time? About eight, might have been quarter past. I suppose Marcus had gone out to get her something from the all-night chemist — she sounded really bad."

"Poor thing."

"But I do need to know," Jean said firmly,

302

"if she's made arrangements for cover while I'm away."

CHAPTER TWENTY

"So Norma does have an alibi," Rosemary said. "Isn't that maddening?"

"Jean would be cross if she knew *she* was the person who gave her one."

"Mind you," Rosemary persisted, "there's still all this Switzerland business."

"Probably to do with money," I said. "It usually is. Anyway, we'll just have to wait until Bob comes back and see if there's been any development we don't know about. He's bound to come back fairly soon. He's very conscientious about work."

Everything seemed very flat, somehow, when I went to the shop. Norma continued to come and go and Jean continued to complain about it and I counted the days until Norma and Marcus would be going to Switzerland and wondered when, if ever, she would let us know that they were going.

"It's been very slack today," Jean said,

"and I don't think it's going to improve now. It doesn't look as if Norma's going to come back. So I'll go to the bank early and then you might as well go home."

On my way I thought I'd call on Mrs. Lyle and have a word with her about the Kipling first editions. Easier, really, to do it face-to-face than on the phone. She was in and seemed pleased to see me — lonely, perhaps, after her husband had died.

"Come in and sit down. Have you time for a cup of tea?" She bustled about in the kitchen and brought in a tray. "I'll just put a bar of the fire on; it's quite chilly today with all this wet weather."

I accepted the tea and a piece of shortbread and told her about the books.

"I think some of them might be really valuable," I said. "And it's a fairly substantial collection, too. I wondered how much you knew about them."

She smiled. "To be honest with you, not a lot. Alfred was very keen on Kipling and just bought the books over the years. He was a great one for secondhand bookshops, you know; wherever we went on holiday, that was always the first thing he looked for! But I don't believe he ever thought about any *value* they might have, so nor did I. I don't think he paid much for any of them."

"I'm no expert," I said, "but I looked up the titles on the Internet and it did seem to me that someone should value them."

"Oh, the Internet — I could never be bothered with all that! Valuable, you say?"

"Hundreds possibly. I don't know."

"Good gracious!"

"I thought that if you weren't aware of their possible value. . . ." I hesitated. "Well, I thought the money might be useful just now."

"Oh, I'm all right — I can manage perfectly well. But nothing for any sort of extravagance." She smiled again. "It's just that I would like to visit my daughter in Australia — she's in Perth, such a long way away, though she has been over here a couple of times, just to show us the children. Then, when Alfred died, she did say how nice it would be if I went over there for a good long visit. But I didn't feel I could. . . ."

"It sounds like a splendid idea," I said. "I'll get the books back and you can get them valued. I can give you the address of a really reliable man."

"That's very kind of you. But I did give them to the charity and I wouldn't want them to think — it might be awkward."

"No, I'm sure that will be fine. I'll bring

them back to you tomorrow or the next day."

"Oh, they'll be too heavy for you to manage. Perhaps Marcus could do it. Marcus Stanley — you know him of course, such a nice man. He took them in for me."

I looked her intently. "Oh really. When was that?"

She thought for a moment. "Quite a while ago. He called in to bring me the program he'd promised me for the Madrigal Society — Alfred and I always used to go. I hoped he'd stop for a chat but he said his wife had one of her bad heads so he had to get back, and he had to go to the shop and pick up her handbag she'd left there. She had to leave in a hurry, he said, because she felt so bad. Terrible thing, migraines, aren't they? Emily, my daughter, used to have them, but she seems to have grown out of them now; people say you do."

"And that's when Marcus took the books?"

"Yes, I'd told him that I wanted to give them to the charity and they were there in the sitting room, so he said that he was going to the shop anyway so he could drop them off. Well, I said wouldn't it be shut — it was getting on for eight o'clock — but he said that was all right because he had Norma's key."

"I see." I got to my feet. "Don't you worry about anything. I'll bring the books back to you myself — I'm sure I can manage them."

I went and sat in the car for a while before driving off. My mind was churning away and I couldn't concentrate on anything but the conversation I'd just had. Finally, I pulled myself together and drove home and phoned Rosemary.

"If Marcus was there that evening, *just* at that particular time, why ever didn't he say so?"

"Exactly." Rosemary sounded as excited as I felt. "He could have killed Desmond. . . ."

"But *why*? What possible motive could he have had?"

"Oh, motive!" Rosemary said impatiently. "There's bound to have been something we don't know about. And there's all that stuff about them leaving — it all fits in. Ring the station now and see if Bob is back."

"It's not evidence," I said reluctantly. "There might be some other, quite innocent explanation."

"For goodness' sake, stop wittering and get on with it!"

So I rang the station and they said Bob

would be back the following afternoon. I rang Rosemary and refused to call Bob at Bournemouth, pointing out that nothing was likely to happen before then, and promising faithfully that I would ring the station when he was back. I tried to put it out of my mind — the animals were being particularly demanding — but I slept very badly and woke up next morning with a headache. Fortunately, it wasn't a day I had to go to the shop. After taking some aspirin, tea and toast, I thought a good sea breeze would be the best cure.

I parked the car in the quiet bit beyond the harbor and stood leaning on the seawall. There was no breeze; it was a still, dismal day with low clouds and the occasional drizzle of rain, the gray of the sea and the gray of the sky merging into one so that there seemed to be no horizon. Not a day to tempt anyone out. I stood, watching the waves breaking on the shingle, one after the other, in a mesmerizing way that I always found soothing. After a while my head cleared and I felt better. I was about to turn and go when I became aware that there was another person a little way away, also leaning on the wall, apparently lost in thought. It was Marcus Stanley. For a moment I didn't know what to do. Then, on an impulse, I went over and greeted him. He turned suddenly, with an exclamation.

"I'm sorry, Sheila. I didn't see you there."

"You looked very far away."

"Yes."

We both turned back and looked at the sea. This part of the beach was sandy and the waves here broke gently, the water creeping up over the sand silently rather than dashing against the pebbles.

"The tide's coming in," Marcus said.

"Yes." There was so much I wanted to say, to ask, but just for the moment I couldn't. All I felt capable of was watching the slow, inexorable movement of the sea. We must have stood there in silence for several minutes until a large herring gull, probably hoping for food, swooped down close to us, shattering the silence with a hoarse cry.

"You're going away, then," I said.

He turned slowly. "Did Norma tell you?"

"She hasn't said anything yet. No, I overheard her making some arrangements. Switzerland, I believe."

"Just at first. I don't know where we'll go from there."

More silence.

"Marcus," I said, "why did you never tell the police that you were at the shop just after eight on the evening Desmond was killed?"

"I . . . I went to collect Norma's bag — she'd left it behind when she was so ill."

"And you very kindly took those books in for Mrs. Lyle."

"So that's how . . ."

"Yes."

"He was alive when I left him," he said.

"So why didn't you tell the police that you'd been there?"

"I was afraid — Norma said — they might think I'd killed him."

"Perhaps," I said, "you were afraid of them knowing that you'd been there just at that moment, the only window of opportunity, you might say, for killing him. Because the poor girl who robbed the till came in and found him dead quite soon after you were there. Of course, she didn't tell the police because she'd been taking money from the till. Nor did Wendy Barlow, who went to the shop even later and saw him dead. *She* just went away again."

"Good God! I didn't know that."

"Yes, unbelievable, isn't it?" I paused for a moment. Then I said, "If they knew you'd been there, at that particular time, the police might have found that *you* had a reason for killing him. Was that it?"

311

He was very silent, a positive silence, as if he was turning something over in his mind, and suddenly I was frightened, though, even at that moment, I told myself that it was silly to be frightened of *Marcus*. A pair of walkers with their rucksacks and their walking poles greeted us as they went by and I relaxed again. Even though it was quiet, this was a public place; there were people here as well as seagulls.

"Was that it, Marcus?" I asked again, more firmly this time.

He seemed to have been holding his breath and now he let it out in a great sigh.

"It's no use; I can't go on like this any longer. You'll tell the police — I can't stop you — and everything will come out. Look," he turned to face me and said urgently, "will you promise not to tell the police anything until tomorrow? Please."

"So that you can get away to Switzerland?"

"No, no, truly, it's not that. It's just that there's something I have to do before . . ." He paused and then said even more earnestly, "Look, I promise I'll tell the police myself tomorrow. I promise!"

I shook my head. "I can't, Marcus — you must see that. You killed someone. I can't —"

"Please let me explain. Listen to me. Please."

"All right."

He took a deep breath. "It happened when we were living in the Midlands, some years ago. I'd been having a few drinks with a client and then I remembered I'd promised to pick up Norma from a meeting. I wasn't drunk, I swear, but I suppose I shouldn't have driven anywhere. But Norma was expecting me. . . ."

"Couldn't you have phoned?"

"I didn't have a mobile — not everyone did in those days, and I was in the car before I realized I could have phoned from the hotel. Anyway, I knew I was late and Norma would have been waiting.

"It was a dark night, had been raining. He stepped out in front of the car — I swear I didn't see him. I heard this awful bump." He shuddered. "I got out and looked at him. He was an elderly man; I couldn't bring myself to touch him but I thought he was dead. It was a quiet street and there was no one about and no phone box that I could see. I panicked. I just got into the car and drove away."

"Did you tell Norma?"

"I had to; I was in such a state when I got there. She drove us home."

"And you didn't tell the police?"

He shook his head. "I wanted to but Norma said not to. She said it wouldn't change things, just make misery for everyone. A few days went by and nothing happened, and then one day the police came to the house. Norma was out, so I answered the door. Apparently someone *had* seen what had happened — they saw it from the front window of their house. The car was right by a lamppost so they could see the number. They took me to the police station and charged me."

"I see."

"Norma got a good solicitor and he said I could probably get off with a verdict of careless driving, but then they spoke to my clients and they confirmed that I'd been drinking with them. The police hadn't Breathalyzed me the night it happened so there was no evidence that I was above the limit, but there'd been a bad case of drunken driving just then — in all the papers — so they didn't give me the benefit of the doubt." He paused. "I got a prison sentence — two years. I deserved it."

"How was Norma?"

"She was wonderful; she stood by me. There hadn't been much in the papers, thank goodness. She moved everything, the house and the business, too. She was wonderful."

"Did she come and visit you in prison?"

"I told her not to — I couldn't bear her to see me there."

"So what has this to do with Desmond?"

"I was in prison in Birmingham. He lived there then. You know how he liked to do all those good works — well, he was a prison visitor. I didn't see him. I was pointed out to him by one of the guards who told him what I'd done, but Desmond obviously didn't think I deserved saving." He paused for a moment, then went on. "It was just before I was released so I never did see him."

"And he recognized you when you came to Taviscombe?"

"Yes."

"But he didn't say anything?"

"No."

"So what changed?"

"It was when he heard I'd been accepted for the council. He was in the storeroom that night when I went to collect Norma's handbag and he went on about it right away. How he'd held back about exposing me because he believed in giving people a second chance, that sort of thing. But now he felt he couldn't stand aside and let me take public office — you know how smug and self-satisfied he was. And then he started on Norma and how we'd both been living a lie and she was as bad as I was and it was his duty to expose us both. . . . I just snapped. You know how they talk about a red mist — well, it wasn't that exactly, but everything went sort of blurred — I honestly didn't know what I was doing. I felt I had to shut him up somehow. There was a knife, just lying there. . . ." He stopped and squeezed his eyes tight shut, as if to blackout the memory. Then he went on more slowly. "I don't think I meant to kill him. I mean, I didn't aim at his heart or anything — I just wanted him to be quiet."

"But he *was* dead?"

He nodded slowly. "Yes. Yes, he was dead. Lying there with his eyes wide open. I pulled out the knife" — he shuddered — "and wrapped it in something — I don't know what. Then I snatched up Norma's bag and ran away. I drove up onto West Hill and hid it in some gorse bushes where no one would find it."

"Did you tell Norma what you'd done?"

"No, she was too ill — I couldn't. Then, when things seemed to go on as normal — no one knew I was there that night — I thought I wouldn't tell her at all. I remembered how awful it had been for her before and I couldn't bear to think she'd have to go all through that again. Worse this time, because it was murder. I suppose that's the real reason I killed him — it wasn't just to keep him quiet at that particular moment. I wanted to be sure he'd be quiet about what he knew forever."

"But you did tell her eventually?"

"Yes. I'd been having bad dreams and got into quite a state. I had to tell her then."

"That's when she made all those plans about Switzerland?"

"She said the police would never make the connection. They'd never imagine we could have any sort of motive for killing Desmond. Our moving to Switzerland could be for business reasons. She had it all worked out. But now, of course." He struck the harbor wall with his hand. "Those damned books!"

"Yes."

We were both silent for a while. He looked exhausted and I was so overwhelmed by what I'd heard that I couldn't say anything. Then Marcus, who'd been leaning on the wall, straightened up. "Now you've heard how it was, can you please, *please* not tell the police until tomorrow? I have one more thing I have to do. Then I promise . . ." He looked at me, not appealingly, but with a kind of despair in his eyes.

"All right," I said reluctantly. "I'll go to the police tomorrow."

When I told Rosemary what had happened, she said, "Can he can be trusted? What makes you sure that he really will do that?"

"You didn't see his face. He looked absolutely defeated."

"But Norma might whisk him away. She's quite capable of it."

"Somehow, I don't think he's going to tell Norma. Anyway," I continued briskly, "I'll phone Bob as soon as he gets back tomorrow afternoon."

But the next afternoon, just as I was about to phone the police station, Foss knocked a glass off the work top and Tris, investigating as usual, cut his leg quite badly, the other one this time, so I spent the afternoon waiting at the vet's until someone could patch him up. I'd just got back and was making myself a much-needed cup of tea when the doorbell rang. It was Bob Morris.

"I was just going to ring you," I said.

"I thought I'd come and tell you in person," he said. "There was a letter waiting for me at the station when I got back. From

Marcus Stanley."

"A letter?"

"Yes. Confessing to the death of Desmond Barlow."

"I see."

"That's not all. There was a report of an accident last night, on the back road leading to Dunster. Marcus Stanley had driven into a tree. At speed."

"Was he killed?"

"No, he's badly smashed up: broken leg and ribs, a serious head wound."

"Have you told his wife?"

"Yes." He paused as if he couldn't bring himself to say the words. "She said, 'He couldn't even get that right.'"

ABOUT THE AUTHOR

Hazel Holt was a personal friend and literary adviser to Barbara Pym, and is Pym's official biographer. A former television critic and features writer, she lives in Somerset, England.

The employees of Thorndike Press hope you have enjoyed this Large Print book. All our Thorndike, Wheeler, and Kennebec Large Print titles are designed for easy reading, and all our books are made to last. Other Thorndike Press Large Print books are available at your library, through selected bookstores, or directly from us.

For information about titles, please call:
  (800) 223-1244

or visit our Web site at:
  http://gale.cengage.com/thorndike

To share your comments, please write:
  Publisher
  Thorndike Press
  10 Water St., Suite 310
  Waterville, ME 04901